"Are you aware there are rumors floating around town," Duke said carefully, "uh, connecting you to a top-tier bronc rider?"

Angie's jaw dropped. Duke saw color splash her cheeks and he regretted saying anything at all.

"The man wants nothing to do with us." Angie scraped back her hair with one hand, showing her irritation. "I have no idea where he even is," she said with fierce finality. But her eyes filled with such a deep sadness that Duke, uncharacteristically, stepped close and wrapped her in a hug.

For a moment, Angie melted against Duke's broad chest. She felt soft and feminine in his arms. But just when he thought she was going to pull him closer, she cleared her throat nervously and squirmed away.

Considering how flustered Angie looked now, Duke thought he probably ought to opt out of joining them for supper tonight. But Angie lit fires in him like no woman had before.

And whether she realized it or not, he suspected the feeling was mutual.

Dear Reader,

Linked stories done by a group of authors are a lot of fun to write. While it involves weeks of getting to know one another's characters and writing styles, the collaboration experience is great. I was lucky enough to know nearly all six authors who share the Harts of Rodeo books, and I always snap up their books knowing they will be good reading. My hope is that all of our readers will love the cowboys/cowgirls in the Hart family and the people they fall in love with as much as we do.

I had a great time working with my fellow authors on this miniseries, and I'd like to thank Cathy McDavid, C.J. Carmichael, Shelley Galloway, Marin Thomas and Linda Warren for making the experience so wonderful. Be sure to follow the series with Shelley's book, *Austin: Second Chance Cowboy*, which is available in October.

I love hearing from all my readers. You can contact me by email at rdfox@cox.net, or by letter at 7739 E. Broadway Blvd #101, Tucson, AZ 85710-3941.

Sincerely,

Roz

Duke:
Deputy Cowboy

ROZ DENNY FOX

HARLEQUIN®
entertain, enrich, inspire™

Recycling programs
for this product may
not exist in your area.

ISBN-13: 978-0-373-75421-2

DUKE: DEPUTY COWBOY

www.Harlequin.com

Printed in U.S.A.

ABOUT THE AUTHOR

Roz saw her first book, *Red Hot Pepper*, published by Harlequin Books in February 1990. She's written for several Harlequin series, as well as online serials and special projects. Besides being a writer, Roz has worked as a medical secretary and as an administrative assistant in both an elementary school and a community college. Part of her love for writing came from moving around with her husband during his tenure in the Marine Corps and as a telephone engineer. The richness of settings and the diversity of friendships she experienced continue to make their way into her stories. Roz enjoys corresponding with readers either via email, rdfox@cox.net, or by mail (7739 E. Broadway Blvd #101, Tucson, AZ 85710-3941). You can also check her website, www.Korynna.com/RozFox.

Chapter One

Dylan "Duke" Adams drove through the silent, shuttered town of Roundup, Montana, in the wee hours of Monday morning, headed home from a summer-weekend rodeo in Wyoming. Because he also served as Roundup's part-time deputy sheriff he eyed businesses along the main street to see they were locked up tight and that side streets were vacant of anyone up to mischief.

Although, the problems of late that he and his cousin Sheriff Dinah Hart dealt with weren't in-town robberies, but worrisome break-ins at outlying ranches.

He'd driven by himself to the rodeo in Sheridan. His twin brother, Beau, and cousin Colt Hart had both gone on to events in other states. Duke had earned good points in Wyoming despite the rank bull he'd drawn. And he felt great. If he made the National Finals Rodeo and won, it'd mean added prestige for him as a champion bull rider and would enhance business for the family ranch.

Still, his ride hadn't been perfect and Beau nagged him to ride midweek in Custer, South Dakota. Beau nagged a lot. He knew Duke had promised Dinah he'd get home to help investigate the string of ranch burglaries piling up—too many for comfort.

Zorro, Duke's German shepherd named for his black face mask, snored away in the backseat of Duke's pickup. The Ford's engine growled as Duke turned down an alley, a shortcut to his parking space outside his ground-floor apartment. As if sensing the change in the engine's tempo, Zorro sat up, yawned and licked Duke's ear.

"Easy, boy, we're almost home." Duke reached back to rub Zorro's ears and immediately winced. He'd forgotten about the injury he'd sustained when he couldn't release his bull rope quickly enough on his final bull. His fingers felt puffier now than when he'd left Sheridan. He should ice his hand down again, but, man, was he beat.

Pocketing his keys, Duke collected his duffel of dirty clothes and emptied it straight into the washer on his way through his back door. He stopped in the kitchen to draw Zorro a bowl of fresh water before heading to his bedroom where he stripped and jumped into a hot shower. Still damp, he fell into bed. Seconds later he heard Zorro pad in and settle on his dog bed. Almost at once the pet Duke had raised from a pup began to snore like a freight train. Duke rolled over, feeling his mind and body relax.

DUKE JOLTED OUT OF A SOUND sleep as his cell phone blared an obnoxious tune Beau had programmed into his phone as a joke. He patted the nightstand then recalled leaving the phone in the pocket of the jeans he'd kicked off at the foot of his bed. The room was black as spades. Zorro bounded up, barking his fool head off, making locating the phone more chaotic.

Shushing him, Duke scrabbled around hunting for his pants. He hit his sore hand on the bedside table and swore roundly. The bedside clock said 4:45 a.m. He'd slept for maybe two hours, he thought, digging out the noisy instrument at last. Any call at this hour meant trouble. "'Lo," he rasped, doing his best to clear his foggy head.

"Duke, sorry to bother you. I'm sure you got in late from the rodeo."

"Dinah?" He yawned in her ear. "It's okay. Where are you at this unholy hour? Who's that yakking in the background?"

"I'm at the ranch. There's been another break-in."

"What ranch?"

"Thunder Ranch," she said. "Aunt Sarah set her alarm for 4:15 a.m. to check on a pregnant mare that's had trouble. She found the barn doors open, called your dad, and Uncle Josh saw how the thieves went in through the back."

"What's missing this time?" Duke asked.

"More saddles. A couple of new bridles Beau crafted. None were as sentimental or expensive as Dad's saddle these damn thieves made off with before, but bad all the same."

"Dang, Dinah, Beau will be sick. He intended to sell the bridles at the Roundup rodeo."

"Yeah, well, there's worse—the horse is gone. Can you come help me calm the family and look for clues? As you might imagine, it's bedlam here."

"I'll be right there." Duke dug underwear out of his

dresser drawer as he digested Dinah's words. "You mean someone stole the pregnant mare?"

"No, the stallion. Midnight. He's not in the pen behind the barn where Ace put him, or anywhere else that we can find. Ace had separated him from Fancy Gal because Midnight had a cough, and she's with foal. He didn't want to risk a chance of her miscarrying."

"Holy horsefeathers!" Duke hopped around on one foot, tugging on clean jeans. "Is that my dad, Ace and Aunt Sarah arguing?"

Dinah lowered her voice further. "Yes. Ace is still peeved that Mom backed Colt's decision to enter Midnight in rodeos. He called Colt on the circuit and read him the riot act. Ace thinks putting Midnight out there to buck will let people see his worth."

Duke rifled through his closet for an official work shirt. "I'll grant you the stallion is worth a mint, Dinah. But the thieves are stupid to take such an identifiable horse."

"I'll let you tell Ace that," she said, sounding unhappy.

"Hang on. I'll be there in fifteen minutes," he said, even though he was dead on his feet.

Typical of Dinah, she said, "Don't break speed limits."

Duke signed off, pinned on his badge, loaded Zorro and jumped in his truck. As far as he knew this was the first time there had been a second break-in at any ranch. The first burglary at Thunder Ranch, pricy items were taken, along with small implements. The full cost wasn't covered by insurance. And the premiums went up. A saddle of Beau's turned up at a secondhand shop way over in Butte. The shop owner identified the piece from photos Duke and Dinah had circulated on the internet. He didn't know who sold him the saddle. He assumed it came from a down-on-his-luck rodeo cowboy.

Duke reached the ranch in time to hear Ace connect with Beau in South Dakota and ask him to check on new bucking entries.

"Stay," Duke ordered Zorro, and the dog dropped to his belly. Duke interrupted Ace with an exaggerated whisper. "Did Dinah tell you I think it'd be dumb for thieves to enter a well-known horse like Midnight on the national rodeo circuit? Maybe in Podunk rodeos, though," Duke added, giving the matter a second thought.

Ace ended his call. "You may be right, Duke. Colt said something similar when I laced into him. He called Leah back and said he wished he could come home and help us hunt for Midnight. He can't. This trip, he and Royce are hauling our bucking stock to two more rodeos, and he knows we need the money."

Duke glanced around at the milling family. Leah and Colt lived on the property in a double-wide mobile home they'd bought a few weeks ago, until they could afford to build a house. She worked as the ranch accountant. Colt, at the ripe age of thirty-two, same as Duke, had fallen head over heels in love with Leah Stockton, a woman he hadn't seen since high school—a divorcée with two kids. Their love affair sent ripples through the family, but was nothing compared to Colt's other bombshell—a confession he had a son he'd never told his mom, his brothers or anyone in the family about. Duke hated those kinds of family upsets.

The mobile home sat a ways from the house and barns, so Leah or the kids likely wouldn't have heard anything, he figured.

Ace, too, had recently married and moved off the ranch. He and Flynn rented Flynn's dad's house. Duke glanced around, trying to re-create the scene. He saw Leah and Flynn, who'd finally begun to look pregnant, deep in conversation with Dinah. His aunt Sarah leaned against the small corral, talking to his dad. Another ranch hand, Gracie, strode away. She probably had chores to start. Duke thought his aunt looked really pale. "Hey, Aunt Sarah, do you have coffee at the house? I didn't get in until 3:00 a.m. I could use some to prop open my eyes."

She perked up as if she needed a mission. "A coffee break will do us all good, Duke. It'll take only a few minutes to brew a pot. I'll bring out a tray when it's done. Leah, do you want me to take Jill and Davey up to the house and feed them breakfast?"

"Oh, please," Leah said, looking grateful. "I saw them peering out the window, wondering what's going on. I'll go get the kids right now."

Spotting Duke, Dinah strode over. "I'm furious at whoever did this. At first I thought it was a sloppy break-in. But they used saddle blankets to cover the interior barn camera and the perimeter one. *Our* saddle blankets, which they stole last time. This time they took Mom's carved wooden toolbox. Something scared them off before they could load the horse head sculpture. But they moved it to the door."

"Are there tire tracks?"

"No. It hasn't rained in a while. If it'd been last month during our deluge, tracks would be easy to spot and follow."

"Have you phoned neighbors?"

"I decided to wait until more were up, but I'll do it

now. I didn't see the sense in rousting neighbors from their beds. Everyone's been on alert, so if anyone saw or heard anything suspicious I'm confident they would have called in."

"I suppose. But the last break-in was a month ago. Enough time for people to let down their guard. And this time they had to pull a horse trailer. I know most folks wouldn't notice if a rig with a trailer passed, but some might wonder at the hour. When do you figure the break-in happened?"

"Between when Ace looked in on the mare around eleven last night and 4:15 a.m. when Mom came out." Dinah opened a case folder, took out her phone and started making calls.

Duke followed Ace into the ranch office where he said Midnight's papers were filed. Ace had kept a list of everyone who'd bid on the horse at auction. Several ranchers wanted Midnight. Ace and Earl McKinley had actively bid against each other.

"We know everyone on this list," Ace said. "Some have had their ranches hit."

"What about Earl? He wanted Midnight almost more than you and Aunt Sarah. Everyone knows there was a rivalry with Uncle John. Could Earl be behind this?"

Flynn, Ace's wife, who had come up behind the men without either of them hearing her, exclaimed angrily, "I can't believe you would accuse my father of stooping so low, Duke Adams! He's honest to a fault, and that rivalry ended when John died. Besides, Dad has moved to Billings."

"Sorry. I knew that, Flynn. It's just these robberies are a black mark against Dinah and me, and no horse has been stolen before. The first few break-ins we chalked up to kids. Now I think they're too clever by far."

Dinah joined them, and Sarah brought in coffee. "I'm taking these thefts personally," Dinah declared, setting down her folder to accept a steaming mug. "So far every theft has been in my jurisdiction."

"There must be something we've missed," Duke muttered, also claiming a mug. "I know Colt thought taillights at the first robbery here were a Dodge pickup. But half the trucks around are Rams." Duke sat at the desk with his coffee and opened Dinah's file. He sifted through pages of her notes. "They rob in our county, but unload their goods halfway across the state. I take it you reached all the neighbors along Thunder Road?"

"All but Rob Parker," Dinah said. "According to his wife, he left before sunup to deliver hay to his leased acreage across town. She'll have him call when he returns."

Duke turned to a clean sheet of paper. "Meanwhile, let's take an inventory."

They worked until noon, rechecking everything in the office, tack room, feed storage and barns, relying on Sarah, Ace and Josh Adams to say what all was missing. Winding down, Sarah and Leah insisted they break for lunch. They all trudged into the big ranch kitchen where the women assembled sliced meat, cheese, bread and tossed a fresh salad while Duke, Ace, Josh and another of the hired hands went back outside to walk every inch of ground from behind the barn where the thieves broke in, to the highway and along the ditches to see if they'd overlooked any small thing.

They hadn't, and it was a glum crew who ate in silence, except for Leah's kids, who chased around with Zorro, giggling and having a good time.

Pushing back, Duke stacked his plate with others who'd finished eating. Standing, he said, "Ace, if you have photos of Midnight, I'll make flyers to blanket the area and post a missing-horse notice on the ranch website."

Leah left the children with Sarah and excused herself to go pay some bills. Duke's dad and Flynn drifted away. Josh had a stake in the ranch, but rarely ventured an opinion unless directly solicited. Duke wished he related to his dad better, but the truth was his twin and their dad had the better rapport.

Duke gathered the photos and prepared to leave just as Rob Parker phoned Dinah. Being up almost eleven hours straight, plus eating, had made Duke so rummy he missed most of Dinah's conversation with the neighbor.

When she clicked off, she beckoned him over. "I had to pull this bit of information out of Rob. He noticed a black horse standing in a field with a donkey and a sorrel mare with a blaze face at Barrington Rescue Ranch. The sun was in his eyes, so he couldn't tell the black's gender. It could be Midnight."

"Angie Barrington wouldn't steal Midnight," Sarah declared. "I volunteer a couple of mornings a week at her shelter. Angie is as sweet as can be. Duke, you've seen her and her son at our Family Friendship Church. She's passionate about saving injured animals, but she'd never steal one."

Ace spoke up. "I treat some of her rescue animals, and I agree with Mom about Angie's integrity."

Dinah twisted her hair off her neck. "It's well-known Midnight was difficult to settle when you first got him,

Ace. Integrity or not, I've heard Angie thinks all rodeo animals are mistreated. Duke, I need to head back to the office. You go to Barrington's and have a look around. If you need a warrant for access, call and I'll bring one out."

Duke hesitated. He did often accompany his aunt to church, so he'd seen Angie there and in town. He mostly ran into the petite blonde at the feed or tack stores, and he found her attractive—really attractive. But he'd die before he would admit that to any of his family. He had heard from guys on the rodeo circuit about Angie's aversion to rodeo riders. Rumor suggested a big-name Texas bronc champion wanted to marry her, but she'd dumped him because he used spurs when he rode. Locals laughed, insisting the joke was on her when she discovered she was pregnant and the guy refused to marry her. Duke didn't know how much of the gossip was true. Crazy stories made their way around the circuit, and were often embellished and retold until no one knew the real truth.

Still, his palms grew sweaty at the notion of waltzing up to knock on Angie Barrington's door. "I didn't get much sleep, Dinah. Can't you as easily swing past Angie's ranch?"

"I could, but Cliff West, who is printing T-shirts for our sponsorship of the rodeo's Wild Pony Race, called to say he has one shirt ready for me to approve. He closes early today, so I need to get going and stop there on my way to the office."

Duke slowly released a pent-up breath. "Oh, fine. I'll go by Barrington's after I hunt up Aunt Sarah and give her some money from the event I won in Sheridan."

"Hey, hey, you won again? Good going," Ace said,

slapping Duke's back. "That ought to leave you sitting in great contention for the finals."

Duke grinned. "Yep. Beau thinks I should hit the next couple of rodeos with him, but he can be such a mother hen, always pushing me to pile up more points."

Ace and Duke fell to discussing bull riding, and Dinah took off. Spotting his aunt emerging from Leah and Colt's mobile home, Duke flagged her down.

She accepted his money on behalf of the ranch, but looked glum all the same. "With Midnight gone, staying afloat until we get some foals will be difficult. I don't have to tell you we paid too much for him, and counted on recouping enough from his foals to pay his loan and then some."

"We'll find Midnight, Aunt Sarah. A horse isn't hockable like saddles or small ranch implements."

"You're right. It's…just that you're all such good kids, you deserve pieces of this ranch one day. I can't believe John wasn't a better steward," she said, bringing up her husband, who everyone in the valley had thought was an astute rancher, but who'd turned out not to be.

"Please don't worry," Duke said. "Well, I'd better go see about the black horse Rob Parker saw at the Barrington ranch."

"If it is Midnight, he broke out and somehow got into Angie's field, Duke, so give her a chance to explain."

"I will." He hugged her briefly, whistled for Zorro, who'd found a spot to lie in the shade, loaded him and left. Duke hadn't the faintest idea how to broach the subject of the horse theft with Angie. He had never been at ease around women he admired. Angie Barrington was no exception.

Scant minutes later, he stared into a fiery sun sink-ing between mountains to the west as he drove down Angie's lane. He kept an eye out for a black horse, but didn't see any animals until he neared her modest ranch house, where chickens scattered at the sound of his truck. Like many older ranch homes, Angie's lane ended at her back door. As a rule visitors went first into the kitchen, the gathering place for rural folks.

Crawling out of his cab, Duke made his way to the house. The door was propped open. He could see Angie working in her kitchen through the screen. He patted Zorro's head, took a deep breath and knocked lightly on the house siding.

ANGIE MADE AND SOLD horse treats for extra cash. She had a batch ready to come out of the oven and another prepared to go in when she heard a knock. Assuming it was someone dropping off a stray animal, she called, "The screen isn't locked, come on in." The hinges squeaked, and Angie glanced up from scooping hot cookies off a large cookie sheet. For a second she was dumbstruck at seeing Dylan Adams poke his ruggedly handsome face into her house. The angle of his cowboy hat hid his eyes, but Angie knew they were a velvety-brown.

"Ma'am," he mumbled, causing all manner of irrational thoughts to run through Angie's addled brain as he swept off his black cowboy hat and gave directions to a big dog to stay outside. Then the man himself stepped inside, seeming to shrink her already small kitchen with his broad shoulders and six-foot height.

She had observed him often at church with his aunt, Miss Sarah Hart. And she sometimes spotted him at the feed store or heading in or out of Austin Wright's

Western Wear and Tack Shop where she sold some of her horse cookies. She thought Dylan Adams was a hunk. And just now he caused waves of heat to sizzle up from her toes.

Mercy, what was he doing here, filling up her kitchen? Grandpa Barrington, from whom she'd inherited her ranch, spoke often of the Hart dynasty. Ace Hart was Angie's vet, and Miss Sarah volunteered to feed and groom her small animals. Colt and his sister, Dinah Hart, and even the cousins, Dylan and Beau Adams, traveled in different circles from Angie. All were hotshot rodeo jocks, and Angie had long since seen through that veneer.

However, of all the clan, Dylan, whom Ace and Austin called Duke, intrigued her. He seemed nice. At church he came across as a gentleman. Truthfully, he was one of the few men near her age in the area that Angie gave a second look. And here she was, up to her elbows in oats and apples, hot, sticky, her hair in a braid—not the impression she'd prefer projecting to a man known to give her heart a hitch and a half.

Recovering enough to close her mouth, Angie quickly slid the remaining cookies off the sheet, shucked her oven mitts and set them aside. "I...ah...assume you've brought me some kind of a stray," she said, fussing with her braid. "If you'll give me a minute to bag the cool cookies so they don't get too hard, and deal with a tray due out of the oven in two minutes, I'll join you outside and see what you've got."

To keep from thinking about how he might judge her messy kitchen and her, Angie set to work bagging and sealing the treats. It crossed her mind that Dylan acted a tad flustered, which surprised her, because he always appeared quiet and collected.

DUKE FELT AWKWARD INVADING this feminine space. Not that he didn't cook, he did. And he'd helped out in his aunt's kitchen, and Dinah's, too. But this was Angie Barrington's kitchen. She had frilly curtains at her windows. And her head didn't reach his shoulder. In a lot of ways she reminded him of Kelly Ripa on TV, except Angie's hair usually hung below her waist. Today, without makeup and with her hair braided down her back, she looked about half his age when he knew darned well she was twenty-nine. His friend Austin Wright had shared that information. Duke often saw her entering Austin's shop, so he'd asked if they were dating. His friend denied it so fast, Duke believed him. Austin said their dealings were all business.

"I'm not in any rush, so take your time." Tired as he was, Duke stretched the truth. Still feeling uncomfortable on the unfamiliar turf, he rolled his hat in his hand and moved closer to her kitchen counter, watching as she placed a gold-and-black logo seal on packages filled with six treats. "Our horses out at Thunder Ranch love these things. I buy them by the case at Austin Wright's shop. I've seen them sell like hotcakes at the feed store, too."

"That's good news. It's a recipe I found in my grandmother's recipe box after I moved here. The side business helps defray rescue expenses. Cookie sales are picking up. I'm considering expanding and hopefully hiring help, so I'm glad your horses love them." She flashed him a smile.

"I didn't bring you an animal," Duke blurted; his

knees melted under her smile, but he owed her an explanation for barging into her home. "There's been another ranch break-in at Thunder Ranch. It's their second."

"Oh, I noticed you were wearing your badge. So, you're out informing neighbors? It's lucky I guess that everyone knows I don't have anything worth taking."

Duke didn't know how to tell her that one of her neighbors said she might possess a stolen horse. "Ma'am," he began, pausing as he fiddled with his hat. "At this ranch invasion thieves made off with an expensive horse."

Angie glanced up, plainly startled. Just as she was about to speak, the screen door banged open and in ran an out-of-breath, sandy-haired, freckle-faced, gap-toothed boy. Excited, the kid stabbed a finger toward the door. "Wh-whose p-pickup and n-neat dog?" he stuttered. "Is it my dad?"

"Lucas, what on earth…!" Angie flushed.

The boy's query had Duke stepping more fully into view. He had moved aside to avoid getting plowed into. The kid's question gave him pause, since all of the gossip Duke had heard indicated the boy's father wasn't now or ever had been in the picture.

"Luke, the pickup and dog belong to Deputy Adams, and he's here on business."

The boy spun and squinted up at Duke. "Mom, he's who brought f-fly-ers to my Sunday-school class." The boy's excited words exploded in a rush. "You know… 'viting kids to be in the wild p-pony race. Did you s-s-sign me up, Mom?"

Pursing her lips, Angie turned at the sound of the oven timer and bent to retrieve two more sheets of cookies. "That's not why Deputy Adams is here. I haven't committed to letting you be in that race, Lucas. Besides, it takes three to make up a team."

"You should sign him up," Duke said, smiling at the boy he felt sympathy for. Duke knew what stuttering was like. He'd been plagued by the problem himself as a youngster, and it still hurt to think about the humiliation of it.

"The Wild Pony Race is good, all-around fun," he said, addressing Angie. "For the past three years the sheriff's office has sponsored the race, which is why I distributed entry packets to various kid groups."

Angie eyed her son with a heavy heart. He had started stuttering last year in first grade. The truth was he got teased a lot, and he hadn't made friends as she had hoped. "We don't have close neighbors," she said for Duke's benefit. "During the school year I clerk in the elementary-school office. Between that, the escalating horse-cookie business and my rescues, I don't have a lot of time for Luke to make playdates. You may recall that my grandfather was ill for some time. His care, the shelter and raising Lucas added up to more than a full-time job." She fussed at the counter full of cookies. Moving the bowl of those still unmade, she said a bit stiffly to her visitor, "Thank you for the community update." Her gaze cut again to her son.

Duke could see she didn't want to worry the boy by mentioning the break-ins. "Uh, I never got around to telling you exactly why I'm here," he said after clearing his throat. "Today a neighbor reported seeing a black horse in one of your fields. If you don't mind, I'll take a look around, since the horse fits the description of the stallion missing from Thunder Ranch."

"You think I…?" She broke off to brace her hands

on her hips. "Listen, Deputy Adams, if that stallion is in one of my fields, he got there without my knowledge. The only black horse I have is an old gelding Carl Peterson found wandering along the road outside his fence line. Obviously the horse got too old to serve any purpose to his former owner, except to cost him for feed. So they turned him out to fend for himself. That's happening more and more in these down economic times."

Duke frowned. "That's terrible." He realized Angie hadn't said someone left the horse to die, but that's what she meant. "I can't believe the insensitivity of some animal owners. Those kinds of fools shouldn't be allowed to own a horse," he ended emphatically.

"I'm glad you feel that way," Angie said. She reached over and shut off her oven, then put the uncooked dough in a walk-in pantry. "I'll finish baking after I give you the grand tour of Barrington Rescue Ranch, Deputy."

"Thank you, ma'am." Duke held open the screen and stepped back to let Angie and her son pass. "Call me Dylan, or Duke," he said. "We do see each other at church and around town."

"It's a deal, if you stop calling me ma'am. Angie will do."

"I l-like Luke, better than Lucas," the boy said, bouncing along. "Your d-dog sni-niffed my hand," he stuttered. "Wh-what's his name?"

"Zorro. Have you seen the movie? Zorro wore a black mask, and my German shepherd has the same look about him."

"Yep," the boy said, squinting up at the tall man. "Hey, w-we rhyme, Duke and Luke. Isn't that c-cool, Mom?" Luke said, giving a little hop.

She darted a sidelong glance at the man walking

Chapter Two

Duke slowed his steps and smiled as he watched Luke playing tag with Zorro. "My dog loves all the attention," he said, waiting while Angie checked the enclosure and the feed trough of a potbellied pig.

"This is Layman. I'm trying to find him a home. There was a time potbellied pigs were considered ideal pets. Once the novelty wore off, and people discovered they really were pigs with just a bit better disposition, a new animal fad replaced them, and they get discarded like old tennis shoes."

"That sucks," Duke grumbled, bending to scratch the fat white pig behind his ears. "Pets are part of the family."

Angie had cut a shock of fresh lettuce from her garden as they walked past. She scattered the leaves in Layman's trough. "Sadly, not everyone believes that," she said, growing serious all of a sudden. "My grandparents ran this animal rescue ranch, but it's grown since I took over. And costs keep rising."

"Ace mentioned he treats your animals."

"I hate calling him, because half the time he doesn't charge me. And bless your aunt for spending time showering love on some of my neediest pets." They walked on to a pen full of goats. "The family who raised these goats had to move when the husband found work in the city. The babies are so cute I can't bear to part with them. I'll probably wish I had when they grow bigger and start being pesky."

"You have an odd assortment," Duke remarked, when a very pregnant donkey lumbered up to the fence. "I would have sworn this was primarily cattle and horse country. Where do these all come from?"

"Oh, people drive out from surrounding towns and dump some off in the middle of the night," Angie said. "Some bring abandoned animals that wander onto their land. I have three sheep from a family whose daughter raised them in 4-H. She went off to college. Her dad is a long-haul trucker, and his wife wanted to go on the road with him. They planned to sell the sheep, but the daughter couldn't bear the thought of sending them off to be lamb chops."

Duke laughed. "You're as soft a touch as Ace, I can tell," he said as Luke ran up followed by Zorro. The boy stuttered his way through telling his mom he wished their two dogs were this much fun.

"Honey, you know the dogs we currently have were mistreated. They're afraid of people. We need to be patient."

"I—I know," the boy said, as he went to his knees and flung both arms around Duke's big dog.

"There's a tennis ball in the backseat of my truck," Duke said. "If it's okay with your mom, Zorro loves to play fetch."

"C-c-can I?" His hazel eyes lit. Duke figured the boy's father must have had brown eyes, because Angie's eyes were almost a silvery-blue.

"You *may*," she stressed, taking time to point out the difference between *can* and *may.*

The adults stood in silence as boy and dog tore back down the path. Duke broke the silence first. "If the only reason you haven't signed him up for the Wild Pony Race is a lack of teammates, I can ask around and see if anyone in his age group is in need of a third person."

Angie clamped her teeth over her bottom lip. "I guess you noticed my reluctance to commit about the race. I'm not being mean. His first year of school was difficult. Two weeks into the school year, practically out of the blue, he started to stutter. Our pediatrician says there's no physical abnormality. He believes Luke will probably outgrow it. I had him tested by the school. When school starts in the fall Luke will meet twice a week with a speech therapist. Call me overly protective, but his condition worsened when other boys picked on him. He's small for his age and, well, I can't risk this pony race being another bad experience for him."

Recalling the difficulties he had with the same problem of stuttering and being teased unmercifully as a kid, Duke nevertheless couldn't bring himself to share such personal information with Luke's mom, a woman he'd like to impress.

"I'm not trying to pressure you," he said, "but I see all the entries and usually hear about kids wanting to sign up. I could pass on names of any seven- or eight-year-olds who need a partner, so you can check them out. There are a lot of good kids in Roundup."

"Lucas has been badgering me since the Sunday he came out of class with that flyer. Okay," she said slowly. "Call if you hear of anyone needing a partner."

Duke sensed she still had reservations.

They meandered on and she stepped off the path to fill a scoop from a bin and then she scattered corn for the chickens. They saw a pair of barn cats slink away from where they hid in weeds to watch the chickens. "Those cats," Angie lamented. "I need to find them homes before my feisty hens give them a lesson they won't soon forget."

Her companion didn't comment, and Angie worried that she was talking too much and was boring him. "We're nearly at the field where I have the horses turned out. I have an old Shetland pony and two gentle mares I rescued from a urine production line selling to a slaughter house. They'll make someone good saddle horses. Ah, there's the old fellow I told you about, plus a younger gelding I rescued from a rodeo-stock contractor who beat him to make him buck."

As soon as they reached the fence, the horses wandered over. Angie had treats in her pockets, and the horses crowded in for their share.

Duke saw the old horse still had prominent ribs, but none of the animals in her care had defeat in their eyes. He liked that.

"The mares look so much better than when the Humane Society turned in the farmer who ran the operation. The Shetland came from an elderly lady's farm. She couldn't feed herself, let alone a pony, a dog and multiple cats."

"I'm sorry to have troubled you," Duke said, withdrawing his hand from the old horse's muzzle. "Color is the only thing this old guy has in common with my aunt's stallion. I'll let you get back to your baking. I really wish Midnight had jumped your fence. Dinah is frustrated because the thefts are getting more frequent, and no one sees anything."

Luke, out of breath from his game of fetch with Zorro, caught up with his mom and Duke as they turned back toward the house. "That was fun," he announced, this time with no stutter. He handed Duke the tennis ball. As Duke tried to close his swollen left hand around the ball, he caught his breath at the sudden pain, and the ball fell and rolled down the path.

Angie saw and automatically reached for his puffy, discolored hand. She examined his injury in the light spilling from an outside barn light that had switched on. "That looks bad, Dylan. What happened? Have you had it x-rayed?" she asked, lightly stretching out his fingers.

Her whole demeanor spelled caring, which Duke found interesting, and sweet. He'd been around half his family for the better part of the day, and no one noticed the swelling. Or if they did they were so inured to rodeo injuries, they had taken his latest injury in stride.

"It happened Saturday at the Sheridan rodeo on my last ride. Haymaker was the bull's name. I knew he was a rip snorter prone to burying his head and twisting midair to dislodge his rider. This was my fault. I wrapped the bull rope too tight around my hand. At the buzzer, I leaped off, but Haymaker spun away. He jerked me around pretty good until I was able to release the rope. Really, it's minor," he finished saying, because Duke certainly didn't want Angie to think he was a wimp.

"Y-you ride b-bulls in the rodeo?" Luke got out, his eyes shining and wide. Plainly awed, the boy danced around Duke, asking more about the rodeo.

Duke noticed Angie purse her lips and settle her

hand heavily on her son's shoulder. "Back to the house, young man. Dylan's leaving."

"But, do y-you know my d-dad?" the boy blurted. "He's in r-rodeo. He rides bucking horses."

Angie stopped dead. "How… Where did you hear that?" she demanded, doing a bit of stammering herself.

Duke took the ball from the boy with his right hand, and motioned Zorro on down the path. It couldn't be more plain that Angie was shocked by her son's knowledge.

He heard her mutter, "Never mind," when Luke said that his gramps had told him. Irritation sparked in Angie's eyes as she herded her chatty son to the house. Suddenly she stopped, turned and called, "Goodbye, Dylan. I hope you find Sarah's horse. I'm sure it's a huge worry."

He tipped his hat. Unsure whether or not she'd even consider entering Luke in the Wild Pony Race now, Duke nevertheless needed to establish if it was a possibility. "So, I'll give you a call if I locate any partners like we talked about," he said, raising his voice so she'd hear. Although she hesitated, Duke saw her nod briefly, and so he said, "You keep an eye out for strangers who may not know you think you have nothing to steal. Log the number for the sheriff's office on your speed dial," he shouted as she was closing the screen door. "Your ranch is isolated. The police number in the phone book will reach Dinah or me."

"I'm good," he heard her say. But, happy she hadn't totally dismissed him over his bull riding, Duke let Zorro into the backseat, slid behind the wheel and drove off. The sun was barely a glimmer, but as he glanced in the rearview mirror he noticed Angie still stood in her doorway, watching him.

"That's a good sign, don't you think, boy?" Duke told his dog. Zorro whined and batted his paw on the back of Duke's headrest.

Feeling the adrenaline drain after his lengthy encounter with a woman he found appealing, Duke admitted he was beat and running on empty. But he couldn't stop thinking, and liking, how he and Angie lingered along the path to her horse field. He felt less constrained around her. Unlike women who gushed over him at rodeos, Angie didn't act coy and she didn't flirt. Neither did she talk down to Luke, or scold him when it was patently obvious she didn't want him asking about his father. And she let the boy get through a sentence without rushing to finish it for him the way Duke recalled happening to him. That was all the more frustrating and only served to make a stutterer stutter more.

He set his phone on the console and switched on the Bluetooth feature. He hit speed dial and listened to it ring twice before Dinah picked up, saying, "Sheriff's Office, Sheriff Hart speaking."

"Dinah, it's Duke. I'm just leaving the Barrington ranch. The black horse Rob saw there is an old gelding. Anything else come in while I've been gone?"

"Not a single lead. It's exasperating. Are you heading home to bed?"

"I thought I'd swing past the Number 1 Diner for their Monday-night special before I go home and crash. Care to join me for supper?"

"Rain check? I'm tired, too, and I still have to type up a report to send to the mayor."

"Okay. I'll come into the office early tomorrow. I

want to make up a flyer with Midnight's photo to tack up around town. I'll make that the first page on the ranch website. And we should get notices out to auction barns, livestock and brand inspectors. Do you think anyone took any video of Midnight when Colt had him at the rodeo? If so, we can post it on YouTube."

"You'll have to ask Colt. I'm happy to let you handle all the techie stuff, Duke. Go eat, we can coordinate our next steps tomorrow. Hey, one last question. Did you think Mom looked okay, or should I worry about the strain this theft may have put on her heart? I don't know much about angina, but someone said it could lead to other heart problems."

"She took the theft of Midnight almost as hard as losing Uncle John's special saddle. It is a blow just when it seemed the ranch might recover from its financial woes. She and Ace have to pay the loan they took out to buy Midnight, even if the horse isn't there to earn his keep. But Ace or Flynn, or Leah would be better able to speak to your mom's health. Last time I saw her before today was two weekends ago when I went with her to church. She referred to the bout of angina as a minor incident. Maybe we should take her at her word."

"I suppose," Dinah said, sounding a bit off stride herself. "When we do find the jerks who stole Midnight, you'll have to keep me from wringing their necks."

Duke laughed. Dinah talked tough, but she had the perfect disposition for her job. She knew Montana law, had grown up in Roundup, but her best trait in Duke's opinion—she accepted people for who they were and looked for good in everyone.

"Laugh, but I want to nail the thieves working over our friends, family and neighbors so bad I can taste it."

"Me, too. I think by upping their timetable they're bound to get sloppy and make a misstep."

"I hope so. Enjoy your club steak on toast and all the trimmings. I'll see you bright and early tomorrow."

Duke clicked off as he pulled up in front of the red-brick diner. They all ate there so often they knew the nightly specials by heart. Tonight his timing couldn't be better. A pickup about the size of his pulled out and left an opening where Duke could keep an eye on his vehicle from inside. "Zorro, be good while I'm in eating and I'll bring you some steak." The dog perked his ears, but he lay back down when Duke opened his door and cracked open a window far enough for Zorro to get his snout out for fresh air.

Sierra Byrne, who owned the diner, hadn't grown up in Roundup, but she'd spent summers in her parents' cabin on the nearby Musselshell River. And she served comfort food, which made her restaurant a hit with ranchers and rodeo cowboys who went for stick-to-the-ribs meals. Men and women alike enjoyed the mining theme. Duke wasn't crazy about the tables with sparkly red Formica tops, but in general the place had a homey feel.

Several people greeted him as he entered and that, too, added to the diner's attraction. Two members of the Roundup rodeo committee hailed him to sit with them. The town's fair and rodeo loomed large in everyone's mind as it was only a few weeks away. Preparation didn't change much from year to year, but every year the committees jockeyed their events enough to claim the current rodeo/fair would be the best one yet. And it did seem to Duke that the fair added more booths, the parade got bigger and motels got booked quicker each year, which was good for the town coffers.

Farley Clark owned a gas station at each end of town. He also stored the movable bleachers at his ranch. Duke supposed Farley wanted to ask him to line up burly cowboys to assemble the bleachers. This evening, Farley and his tablemate, Jeff Woods, wanted to discuss the most recent robbery.

"Heck of a note," Farley said, "Sarah and Ace losing that pricy stud. Thunder Ranch being hit twice puts me in mind that whoever's doing this is thumbing their nose at Dinah. What's she got in mind to do? Are there any leads at all?"

Duke shook his head. He hadn't expected to get grilled about the burglary, or he probably would have skipped coming here. Not everyone in town had favored the idea of Roundup electing a woman sheriff. Farley had been one of the most vocal, and had supported Dinah's opponent.

"I'll take the special, with iced tea," Duke called to Susie Reynolds, the waitress heading toward him. She gave him a thumbs-up, and turned back to deliver his order.

"You figure it's a local?" Jeff asked, peeling the label off his bottle of sarsaparilla.

"Bound to be," Duke answered. "Or else someone has spent a lot of time working out escape routes. They strike at night. Nobody hears or sees them make a getaway. Pete Duval's ranch isn't easy to find in broad daylight. Practically all of the ranches hit own dogs who haven't barked in alarm. Dinah and I assume it's guys who know the back roads and local ranch layouts."

Farley Clark stirred two packets of sugar in his coffee. "Did you check at the bank if anyone is making deposits over and above what's normal?"

"Dinah did." Duke watched the man drink the syrupy black stuff. "Farley, these guys haven't left any tracks. You know, I sort of sense you aren't happy with the job Dinah and I are doing. If you want to call a town-hall meeting to let everyone vent, I won't object and I'm sure Dinah won't. We keep hoping someone saw or heard something, but haven't connected it to the break-ins, or didn't think to report it. Remember, Thunder Ranch has suffered the biggest losses. Surely you don't believe Dinah and I wouldn't round up this gang if we could?"

Farley didn't back off. "I'm just saying it's gone on longer than any problem the city's ever had. If Dinah doesn't catch the culprits before our upcoming fair and rodeo, no one will be comfortable leaving their ranches while they attend scheduled events."

Duke's meal came and saved him from losing his temper and snapping at Farley. Susie slipped Duke a small plastic bag. "For Zorro," she said. "I know you always take him some of your steak."

"Hey, thanks. I didn't realize I was so predictable."

"It's okay. I really wanted to come ask if any of your family has heard from Tuf? My older brother is finally back in the States. He's at Kāne'ohe Bay in Hawaii, but he served with Tuf in Afghanistan and asked about him when we spoke. I said I haven't seen him around town."

Duke stopped cutting his steak. "Aunt Sarah has been in contact with him. That's about all I know. But when I'm not at the sheriff's office or out doing that job, I'm off at rodeos." Duke gave a casual shrug. Really he knew everyone in the family worried about his youngest cousin. But they were tight-knit, and not prone to blabber personal stuff that could lead to gossip.

Jeff ordered another soft drink. Luckily Farley took out his money clip, peeled off a tip and dropped it beside his plate. Susie went to help a new customer as Farley said, "I don't think we've reached the stage of calling for a town-hall meeting, Duke, but I wonder if Dinah shouldn't deputize a couple of guys at least through our fair and rodeo. It so happens my son, Rory, is home from college for the summer, along with his good friend, Tracy Babcock. They could be of help. My wife wants Rory to be a lawyer even though he thinks he'd rather be a rancher. A summer internship as a deputy would look good on his résumé if he chooses law."

Now Farley's entire complaint came into focus for Duke and made more sense. "I'll pass that information along to Dinah when I see her in the morning," Duke said. He could almost predict her reaction. Farley's wife had spoiled their only son, Rory, with ready cash, hot cars and expensive clothes only dudes would be caught wearing, and his good buddy, Tracy Babcock, was cut from the same cloth. To keep from further comment, Duke cut a slice of steak and put it in his mouth. He gestured goodbye with his fork as Farley ambled off.

Jeff, who ran a dry-cleaning establishment in town that catered to single cowboys, saw through Duke's badly concealed attitude. "Farley and Janine have high expectations for Rory. The problem as I see it is they've waited too long to clamp down on the kid. I doubt Dinah needs to worry about hiring the boys. Those two and their pals are more interested in partying the summer away with their girlfriends over in Musselshell." Jeff finished his second sarsaparilla, got up, said his farewells to Duke and stopped to talk to a couple of ranchers on his way out.

Duke tucked into his food. His mind lingered less on Farley's desire to have his son play deputy, and more on the nearness of the event under discussion. He thought of his offer to find a team of wild pony racers for Angie Barrington's son. He discovered he liked thinking about Angie. Her efficiency in the kitchen left him wondering how much time she spent making her horse treats. The way he'd seen horses gobble up the oat cookies, they probably ate them faster than one woman alone could bake. If Angie wanted to expand and hire people to help mix and bake the cookies as she'd indicated, she could build a profitable company. He could help her advertise by building her a website—if she'd let him.

Having eaten his fill, Duke sliced and bagged his leftover steak for Zorro. Putting his tip on the money Farley and Jeff had left, Duke got up to go.

Weaving through tables still occupied by people he knew well got him sidetracked by several men who wanted news of the latest robbery. Everyone expressed concern and asked him to pass on good wishes to his aunt and Ace. Thankfully no one else hinted that he and Dinah weren't doing their job.

Outside at last, Duke opened his pickup and let Zorro out. Exhausted as Duke was, Zorro deserved to stretch his legs, and deserved to eat his steak treat in comfort.

The big dog nosed the bag. Whimpering eagerly, he pawed Duke's leg.

"Good dog. But let's walk down to the park before I feed you. I can stand to walk off some of that big meal before I go home and crash for the night."

In spite of the fact it had gotten quite dark in the time

Duke spent in the diner, five or so teenagers still played pick-up basketball in the park. Their only light came from streetlamps set in every block along the town's main street. Pausing at a park bench, Duke braced a foot on the bench seat and he watched the boys shoot hoops as he fed Zorro bits of steak.

Lighting the play areas in the park had been on the town council agenda for at least the four years Duke had served as deputy. The money never seemed to stretch far enough. The mayor insisted, rightfully so, that funding for police, firefighters, trash collection and other essentials came before lighting the park. But watching the kids who finally gave up trying to see the baskets and took off for who knew where, Duke thought it would be money well spent to get park lighting on the next general-election ballot. Not that he was political.

He chuckled over the notion as he fed Zorro the last bite of steak. He imagined Ace asking him when he had turned into such an adult as to be considering funding, politics and other grown-up things.

In Duke's eyes, Ace always seemed more mature than his other cousins. Of course, he'd become the man of the ranch after his dad died. Even before that Duke had gone to Ace with problems Duke's own dad ignored.

He threw the empty plastic bag in a trash bin, then rounded up Zorro and returned to the pickup. In a reflective mood, Duke wondered if he'd given his dad enough credit for keeping him and Beau in food, clothing and a roof over their heads. Perhaps his dad didn't have time to be demonstrative.

At the Ford, Duke loaded Zorro. He saw the sheriff's office across the street was dark except for one interior light they always left burning. Dinah must have finished her report and gone home. The weight of this investigation was on Dinah's shoulders even though she was younger than him by three years. She and Angie were the same age. That thought just popped into Duke's head.

Driving home he compared the two women. Dinah had spent some rocky years before she dug in and turned her life around. Angie hadn't grown up in Roundup. Duke had no idea about her background other than gossip and rumors floating around about her and the Texas cowboy—a relationship that culminated in her having a baby at twenty-one, which left her a single mom with a lot of obligations.

As Duke pulled down the alley and parked outside his apartment he admitted he wanted to know more about Angie. Funny, he never thought he'd spend so much time wishing he knew every little detail about how a woman had grown up. He had spent his early years as a loner. Mostly due to his stuttering he had holed up reading, or watching TV. Old John Wayne movies were his refuge. He watched them so many times it was how the family came to call him Duke, after the star.

Actually, he hadn't minded. The Duke set a good example for a gangly kid who longed to be easier in his skin than he was.

In the kitchen, he filled Zorro's bowl with kibble and gave him fresh water, which about maxed out his energy in this really long day.

Taking a hot shower, he toweled off and crawled between cool sheets, and was oh-so-tempted to switch off his phone lest some new debacle in the normally

placid town forced Dinah to roust him. Not that he'd
ever shirk his duty on a job he took seriously—a job
he loved. In fact if the town ever had money to hire a
full-time deputy he'd lobby for the job.

He fell asleep speculating about what opinion Angie
Barrington had for law officers. He'd pretty much left
her today with the notion rodeo competitors were at the
bottom of her list of desirable men.

Chapter Three

Duke woke up with sun streaming in his bedroom window, and he felt happily refreshed. Fading from his sleep-logged mind—an appealing picture of Angie Barrington smiling at him as she leaned over a corral feeding her horse treats to the magnificent, now-missing black stallion, Midnight.

He planted his feet on the floor and almost landed on Zorro, who lay not on his bed but on Duke's bedside rug, something the dog had done as a pup before Duke bought him his own big, soft bed.

"Sorry, Zorro," he muttered, hopping over the yawning animal to rummage in his closet. He gave up and retrieved a wrinkled shirt out of the dryer. Doing laundry was at the top of his hate list. If it wasn't so expensive he'd drop everything at Jeff Woods's Dry Cleaners. He knew plenty of single cowboys who did. Their jeans and shirts were always pressed and neat. But his part-time job covered rent, food and gas. Since the ranch fell on harder times, those in the family who finished in the money at rodeos, which was almost all of them, contributed what they could toward the ranch. His aunt juggled expenses. She had leased out some prime grazing land. In this part of the country, land was gold. Unfortunately empty acres didn't put money in the bank.

When he wasn't on duty he always wore jeans and black T-shirts. The family teased him for that quirk, too. But he liked black and it was a matter of convenience. Now he stopped to wonder if Angie would find him dull because he didn't gravitate to flamboyant Western shirts like most other cowboys wore.

Still mulling that over in the kitchen, Duke opened the fridge and discovered his milk had gone sour. He spat in the sink a few times, dumped the carton and washed the smelly stuff down the drain. He settled for a breakfast of scrambled eggs and toast, and drank water.

Suddenly, for no real reason, he remembered telling Angie he'd find a couple of kids for her to vet as possible pony-race partners for Luke. He got out the church directory and ran down the list of members as he ate. None of the families listed who had kids the right age jumped out at him.

Rethinking yesterday's conversation with Angie, Duke wasn't 100 percent certain he wouldn't be wasting his time. She sure didn't seem thrilled about the idea of Luke entering. Duke felt slightly guilty at the thought that he'd volunteered so it'd give him a reason to contact Angie again.

Was that pathetic? He needed an excuse to phone or approach a woman that interested him? If it was Colt—well, Colt before he got married—or Beau, those guys were never shy when it came to chatting up attractive women.

Polishing off his breakfast, Duke rinsed the dishes and the pan he'd used to scramble eggs, and put them in the dishwasher.

He tidied up and still found himself replaying comments Angie's son had made about his dad. Angie had cut the boy off quick enough. But Luke kept pressing. Duke wondered if that might make Angie reconsider getting back together with the guy. How similar was her case to Colt's having a kid he had no part in raising—a boy now almost a teen? Colt paid support, and just recently decided he'd like a relationship with his son—Evan was his name, who had a stepdad. Man, relationships could get messy.

Having told Dinah he'd be at the office early, Duke grabbed his hat and whistled to Zorro. He could speculate from now to kingdom come and still have no answers as to the real situation between Angie and her son's birth daddy. And the truth of the matter was he had more to worry about than the Barringtons' family situation. He had a string of robberies, the most recent of which left his family missing a very pricey horse. He locked the apartment and drove into town.

MONDAY NIGHT LUKE HAD RATTLED on nonstop—and he started in again this morning—begging Angie to sign him up for the Wild Pony Race. She was glad Dylan Adams had been discreet in volunteering to hunt up an age-appropriate team in case he didn't find one. The deputy might even forget. He may only have used it as a cover because he'd all but accused her of horse thievery. Someone driving along the road saw her old black horse and told the sheriff, he claimed. But it was embarrassing to think anyone who knew her would even suggest dishonesty in any way, shape or form.

The sheriff probably had to be tough to get elected to that job. Angie only ever saw Dinah Hart at a distance or driving her patrol vehicle. They were about the same age, Angie knew from something Austin Wright said. Well, it didn't matter how many townspeople thought she'd steal a horse, she never would.

And none of that addressed the issue of her allowing Lucas to chase off after some wild pony during a rodeo—which brought up another point. It pained her to think her grandfather had gone counter to her express wishes to not tell Luke anything about his father.

Angie considered Carter Gray a sperm donor at best, and a reluctant one at that. As if she'd gotten pregnant on purpose to hold on to him—to tie him down. He'd pursued her for a year, not the other way around. Oh, who cared? It was all ancient history. Carter had wanted a cook, a housekeeper and a bedmate was all. He hadn't wanted a wife and he sure as heck never wanted a child. Gramps knew that. It must have had something to do with how ill he'd been with pneumonia last winter. Sick enough for the fever to let him ramble. So sick, a third round of antibiotics didn't cure him.

How could she in good conscience blame a sick man, who in her hour of desperate need had opened his home and his heart to her and her unborn child? The answer was, she couldn't. She'd have to negotiate Luke's questions about his dad as best she could. It was just a shame the seed had been planted to make him want something that could never be.

"Mom!" Luke raced into the kitchen from the living room where he'd asked to eat his breakfast cereal while watching TV. "Guess what. Guess what," he shouted.

Angie sighed. "What, Luke?" Of late he never went anywhere at less than a run, and he couldn't seem to talk without his voice bouncing off the ceiling. The one positive thing she had noticed: when it was the two of them alone, he stuttered less. Angie continued to mix cookies. She had one more batch to bake to fill the last of her orders in town. As well she hoped to make another batch to sell at the roadside stand out at the county road along with her tree-ripened apples, farm-fresh eggs and an excess of summer squash. Every little bit extra she earned helped pay growing food costs for her rescued animals.

"On TV they have p-p-pictures of last year's Wild P-pony Race. Come quick and see how fun it'll be."

His eyes glowed with excitement, so she couldn't ignore his request. She followed him to where, sure enough, kids about his age in jeans, plaid shirts with numbers on their backs, and some wearing hats too big for their heads, were clinging to a long rope hooked to a pony's hackamore. The children were being dragged through dust and dirt and, heavens, in some cases, mud. Oh, boy, this was not a ringing endorsement for something she wanted her young son to do.

"And Duke and his dog are there. S-see, Mom? Duke grabbed the pony and s-s-stopped him. The other g-guy said to win, one of the three kids has gotta get on the pony before he crosses that wh-white line."

In his excitement, Luke talked too fast, and so began to stutter some.

"C-can I please sign up? Please, Mom!"

Angie loved him so much. But seeing the arena with lanky cowboys ringing the corral, hearing the roar of the rodeo crowd sent her reeling back to when watching the slapping, hitting, prodding of animals to get them to run, to buck or perform sickened her. Back to a time when the man who she thought loved her had promised to quit the rodeo circuit even though he never had the slightest intention of doing so. All of it caused Angie's head to spin.

"We'll see, Luke," she said, wishing she lived in a town that didn't live, eat, sleep and breathe rodeo. "I need to ask more questions, and really find out how safe it is before I'll agree." She felt relieved to see the station had gone on to show a row of booths at the fair portion of the weeklong affair. All the same, it hurt her to watch the slump of Luke's skinny shoulders, and see him plop down in dejection, the light extinguished from his eyes.

DUKE SHOVED OPEN THE DOOR to the sheriff's office with the elbow connected to his injured hand as he juggled two cups of hot coffee he'd picked up at the convenience store on his way into town. The office he shared with Dinah was little more than a hole in the wall large enough for two desks and a divided jail cell stretched side by side across the back. Two three-drawer filing cabinets separated the desks, and a few Wanted posters hung off a corkboard attached to one wall. Early as it was, Dinah already sat at her computer, but her desk was also strewn with papers, and there were telltale signs she'd already eaten a Snickers bar.

"Oh, I could kiss you," she said, jumping up to relieve Duke of one steaming foam cup. She bumped his hand and he drew back with a moan.

"What did you do?" She narrowed her eyes at his still-swollen hand.

"Don't tell Ace or my dad. I wrapped the bull rope too tight and couldn't release it fast enough at the end of my eight-second ride. The bull whipped me around.

I'm lucky it didn't yank my elbow or shoulder out of a socket."

"Will this injury jeopardize your point standing? Do you have to scratch an event?"

"No. It feels better today and my next rodeo isn't until the weekend. I see you're reviewing previous robberies. Anything new? Anyone call the tip line?"

"No calls since you phoned last evening to clear Angie."

Duke sat at the second desk and turned on his computer.

"Rob Parker's tip about seeing a black horse there gave me hope," Dinah said. "Now we're back to square one, darn it."

"Angie's ranch is definitely a dead end. I insulted her by the mere suggestion she'd harbor a stolen horse."

The pair sat in silence a moment, sipping their drinks, each deep in thought. With Duke's mind having reverted to Angie, he set down his cup, leaned forward and suddenly asked, "Dinah, do you know of any eight- to ten-year-old boys hankering to get in the Wild Pony Race but may need a third to make a team?"

Spinning in her chair, Dinah scrutinized Duke. Her keen mind always worked overtime. She laughed and poked him. "Angie has a son about that age. You wouldn't be going soft on her, would you, coz?"

Wanting to hide his interest in Angie, Duke met Dinah's probing eyes. "She has a cute kid, who happens to have a stuttering problem to which I can relate. I gathered he hadn't made many friends last year in first grade. The boy, Luke is his name, got the flyer I handed out to his Sunday-school class. He wants to sign up in the worst way, but as you can imagine, his stutter-

ing probably hinders other kids from including him. I
thought I'd check around a bit is all."

"Gosh, I'm sorry to hear about his problem. Sorry for
Angie, too, even though I don't really know her." Dinah
removed the lid from her cup and blew on the hot coffee. "Hmm, I just had a thought. Gary and Pam Marshall have twins who I think will be in second grade this
fall. Tommy Marshall is a bit of a hellion. His brother,
Bobby, is a nice, sweet kid. Last week I saw Pam at the
library and she hadn't yet signed the boys up to race.
I'm pretty sure she said they lacked a third kid. Call
her or Gary."

"Thanks, I will." Storing the information in his head
to check into later, Duke accessed his computer copy of
Dinah's break-in file. "You know, like I said yesterday,
horse thieving doesn't fit the pattern we've assembled
on our crooks. Everything else points to them being
petty thieves. In all except this last robbery, they've
taken items easily pawned or sold to secondhand shops."

"True, but Ace knows he put Midnight in a pen behind the barn when he checked the laboring mare at
eleven."

"If Midnight accidentally got out I'd expect to find
him in the field with the broodmares."

"Ace checked there first. I've gone over and over
every step we've taken to date. We've been thorough,
Duke."

"That's what I told Jeff Woods and Farley Clark at
the diner last night. Farley suggested you deputize his
son, Rory, and his buddy Tracy Babcock. He seemed
to think with adding boots on the ground, so to speak,
you'd solve the case in no time." Duke tossed that out

obliquely, but wrinkled his nose as Dinah's mouth fell agape.

"I hoped you were kidding, but I see you're not. Does Farley know we start work before noon?" she said caustically. "I hear Rory doesn't get up before then."

Duke laughed. "Jeff said not to worry. Rory and his pal are too into partying with their girlfriends to want to work. I felt I had to warn you in case Farley takes his idea to the mayor."

"Ah, well, the mayor will nix it quick. He's in budget meetings with the city council all month. The last meeting someone suggested replacing all our rodeo/fair banners. The mayor went on for twenty minutes how there's not one extra cent in the city's discretionary fund."

"In a way that's a relief." Duke glanced at the case file again. "What we have so far is this. The thieves know this area. They're night owls. And they're growing bolder."

Dinah let out an exasperated sigh. "At first they lifted stuff they could toss in the back of a pickup. Now they have a horse trailer. A covered one, I assume, to conceal a distinctive horse."

"If you want to follow up on leads where they may have unloaded the last custom saddles of Beau's, Dinah, I'll concentrate on getting word out to places where they could sell a horse," Duke said. "I'll email Midnight's photo to Beau and Colt. Ace gave me a detailed description for livestock inspectors and auction barns. I'll check online newspaper ads for private horse sales. What do you think about starting a blog we can hitch on to some well-known trade bloggers?"

"Great. But you do remember I'm registered for a

professional development class in Billings the first week of August? I need to leave Sunday as workshops start early Monday. I can cancel if it conflicts with any of your scheduled rodeos. Your point standing to make the NFR is more important than my class."

Duke took out his BlackBerry. He liked bull riding, and this year had his sights set on getting to and winning at Finals. He also wanted to catch these crooks.

"I'll make Bozeman this weekend. I can skip Great Falls the days you're talking about. Beau never misses that rodeo."

"You're twins, but it's not as if you're interchangeable in vying for the Finals. Beau isn't in the running. You are."

"Beau could be in contention. He's the better rider," Duke said offhandedly.

"Huh? Are you afraid he'll beat you if you compete against him?"

"No. But, believe it or not, he doesn't ride his best when we're up against each other."

"As gung ho as he is to succeed at everything? Although, I have noticed he tends to push you. You've gotta stop letting him do that."

"I don't *let* him, Dinah."

"Well, you sometimes hang back. Why would Beau *let* you win, Duke?"

Duke wondered about that himself. "I agree it makes no sense. But the upshot is, I can easily skip Great Falls. You take your class. I hope you learn new tricks for tracking ranch robbers and horse thieves if we haven't solved this case by then."

"We have to find Midnight soon. The ranch can't afford to absorb the cost of his monthly loan payments if he's not standing at stud. What that means is Colt and the hands taking stock to more rodeos, which leaves Ace doing double duty. He wants Tuf to get home."

"Speaking of Tuf… Susie Reynolds asked about him. I pled ignorance because I know Ace thinks he's shirking. Really, what is up with Tuf?"

"I can't imagine why he got out of the Corps and hasn't come home. Mom said he told her he needs time. She's okay with it. But it irritates Ace."

"Maybe Tuf does need time. We can't begin to understand the hell he's been through."

"You mean, maybe he's injured and doesn't want us to see him like that?"

"Your mom wouldn't be okay with that. I mean the expectations of this family can be overwhelming. Maybe Tuf needs breathing room."

Dinah looked unhappy. "If he can't breathe on four thousand acres in the middle of Big Sky Country, he can't breathe anywhere."

"Pardon me for saying so, Dinah, but your attitude is a bit of what I mean about family expectations. Tuf may not be up to everyone demanding a piece of him."

"We love him. He'd be better off decompressing with us. He should know that."

Duke left it at that, and each fell silent until the phone on Dinah's desk rang. "Sheriff Hart," she answered briskly, then grabbed a pad and scribbled on it.

"What's shaking?" Duke asked when she hung up and left her chair all in one motion.

"A car went into the ditch on the approach to the covered bridge. No injuries. I can handle this alone if you want to finish the flyer and start the blog we discussed."

"Should I call for a wrecker?"

"Let's wait and see if I can pull the car back on the road with the front winch on my patrol SUV."

"Okay. If you're not back by the time I have the flyer done, I'll lock the office and start tacking them up. I may run some out to the two auction barns east of town while I'm at it, and finish up the other half of town in the morning."

"It's a plan. When you send Colt and Beau copies on their iPhones, ask them to print off flyers and pass them around as they travel home."

"Will do. The thieves aren't dumb enough to try and sell Midnight locally. Frankly I wish they were stupid."

Being a perfectionist, it took Duke longer to set up a flyer than it should have. He agonized over writing the blog because he didn't want it too wordy. But he also didn't want it to be boring.

Dinah checked in once to say she wasn't able to winch the out-of-towner's van out of the ditch. It had broken an axle. "The driver tells me a feed truck passed him too close and forced him off the road. I'm trying to figure out who's at fault. We have a gazillion ranchers hauling grain this month," she said. "No one in the van got a license plate number."

"That would make your job too easy," Duke teased. "That's why Roundup pays you the big bucks."

She gave a snort and disconnected. Duke decided he needed a break from the computer and stepped outside to get some air. Zorro had been cooped up with him all morning. He needed the bushes planted between buildings.

Glancing up as he stood waiting for Zorro to do his business, Duke was surprised to see his dad emerge from the Number 1 Diner. "Hey, Pop," he called.

Josh ambled over to join him.

"It's unusual to see you in town this time of day. Is everything all right with Aunt Sarah and the ranch?"

"I ordered pipe fittings for the irrigation system. They came in, and Sarah asked me to pick up a few things at the store. I wondered if you or Dinah were in the office. I planned to stop by before heading home. Any updates on the robberies?"

"No. Dinah is out on a call. I put out an internet flyer on the horse. And I printed some off to post around town. I came out to take a break from writing a blog to send out to online trade magazines."

"That stuff is all Greek to me."

Zorro loped to the curb where the men stood. The arrival of a bus that came through once a week forced them to step back to keep from being in the way of the pneumatic door when it opened.

Zorro's ears perked and he growled low in his throat. At first Duke thought it was the hiss of the door upsetting his pet, but then he saw the driver assisting a slender woman with short, silvery-gray hair down the steps. Along with her wheeling suitcase, she held the handle on a harnessed service dog. The woman thanked the driver and asked a question in too soft a voice for Duke to hear.

Josh seemed rattled by the incident, and he wore a funny look as he watched the woman and dog cross the street to where they entered the diner.

"Do you know that blind woman, Pop?"

"A long time ago," his dad murmured, appearing totally distracted. "I need to go, Duke. Let Sarah or Ace or me know if you get any leads on Midnight," he said as he rushed off. He recrossed the street behind the bus as it pulled out in a cloud of exhaust.

Duke wound his fingers in Zorro's collar because he strained at his leash. It was more than odd to see his dad hurry back into the diner he'd left moments ago. If his dad intended to run after the woman, it was even stranger. In all the years their dad had been single, Duke had never known him to look twice at any available women his age in town. Duke assumed he was a one-woman man who never got over losing their mother. In fact, he liked that idea.

Slightly off-kilter himself, Duke went back inside the office and sat down to finish his project. But his mind kept revisiting his dad's behavior. By the time he sent the piece off, he began to think about what surely must have been a lonely existence for a man raising twin sons alone. His thoughts leapfrogged back to Angie Barrington. Numerous times during the day she'd invaded his thoughts for no reason. He shut down the computer and put a stack of flyers in a manila folder.

Well, he did have reason to think of her. He'd promised to see if he could find a Wild Pony Race team for her son. And depending on the route he took to pass out his flyers, one direction would take him right by Gary and Pam Marshall's ranch. Dinah's suggestion to ask about their twins was more viable than any he'd come up with.

Chapter Four

Duke posted flyers in town. Many times he had to tack it above or below notices advertising Roundup's fair and rodeo.

A couple of bystanders asked him if the family planned to post a reward for information leading to the return of Midnight. Eyeing them speculatively, Duke said that hadn't come up as they assessed all the items stolen from the ranch. Then he asked what they knew about the robberies, but didn't get any answers.

Cal Benninger, a crotchety cattle rancher, groused about the lack of a reward. Duke was quick to point out that the Hart clan and others had congregated to render aid a dozen years back when Cal's youngest son needed rescuing from a fall down an old, unmarked copper mine shaft. "That's neighbor helping neighbor because it's right," Duke stressed. "No reward necessary."

"Not the same thing," Cal said. "A family member is different than that expensive stud Sarah and Ace bought for the purpose of making a profit."

Duke let that go and climbed in his pickup to head on down the road. He knew times were tough, but he hoped not everyone agreed with Cal. Still, he made a mental note to ask Dinah if she thought offering a reward might jog memories.

He tacked up a flyer on a pine tree across from the lane that went into the Marshall ranch. Pam Marshall answered Duke's knock while wiping her hands on her bibbed apron. "Duke. It's a surprise to see you this far out of town," she said as he ordered his dog to sit. "We heard about the latest robbery at Thunder Ranch. In June, Gary installed five-hundred dollars' worth of perimeter lights. He got nervous after the Jacksons next door lost tools and tack adding up to several thousand dollars."

Duke removed his hat. "We know theft costs are mounting. I'm actually not here about the break-ins, Pam. Dinah said your boys might want to compete in the Wild Pony Race. Do you know Angie Barrington? She's considering signing her son, Lucas, up, but she's not fully comfortable and would like to talk to moms of possible teammates." He hadn't finished his sentence when two boys, one about Luke's size and the other taller and heavier, squeezed past on either side of their mom. The smaller of the two boys knelt to pet Zorro. The bigger boy squinted up at Duke. "Luke Barrington is a squirt and a loser."

The boy's mother delivered a stern look. The smaller boy puffed up. "Tommy, Luke can't help that he stutters. 'Sides, he's no squirtier than me."

Duke had already figured the mouthy kid was Tommy Marshall based on Dinah's earlier depiction of the twins. A twin himself, Duke was well aware twins could be as different as night and day. He did wish Tommy Marshall was more like his brother.

"I've met Angie, uh, Ms. Barrington," Pam declared.

"She works in the school office. You boys like her. Tommy, you appreciated her giving you a ride home last year when it snowed in April and my Jeep had a dead battery."

"Yeah, she's nice," Tommy admitted. "But Luke can't even bat a ball."

Bobby intervened. "He tries. Come on, Tommy, we wanna be in the pony race and every guy we've called so far has three on their team."

Tommy shoved his brother's hand away. "Yeah, but I want to be on the team that wins."

His mother cautioned Tommy again. "If you can't change your tone, young man, your dad and I may decide you can forget the whole thing."

Duke saw the chance for Luke slipping away. He decided on a spur of the moment to sweeten the pot. "If you three team up, I'll make time to take you out to Thunder Ranch, bring in some ponies and teach you how to work together to get one of you on the pony before he crosses the finish line. Winning takes concentration and team work. Most kids start out okay, but they get hyper and trip over each other."

"Deputy Adams is a champion bull rider," Bobby told Tommy.

"I know. I've seen pictures of him, his brother and his cousins hanging in our veterinarian's office."

"Your vet is my cousin Ace," Duke said. "He won buckles at a lot of rodeos. We all have. So, what do you say, guys? Do we have a deal if your mother and Ms. Barrington talk it over and agree?"

Tommy hitched up his pants. "I'll do it if I get to be the one who rides the pony."

"It's not settled, Tommy," Pam said. "Your father and

I will discuss it. If he's okay with it, I'll phone Angie."
She had been frowning at the top of Tommy's head, but
glanced up and offered Duke a tired smile. "Either Gary
or I will let you know in the next day or so, Duke. Well,
I'd better get back to canning green beans," she said.

"Green beans—gross!" the twins exclaimed in uni-
son.

"Thanks, Pam," Duke said. "I told Angie I'd get back
to her with a possibility. So don't be surprised if she
calls you first."

"Oh, good. I want to order a bushel of apples from her
anyway. And, Duke, good luck tracking those thieves."

He settled his hat on his head. Opening the Ford's
door, he let Zorro climb into the backseat. As he got in
and revved the engine, he couldn't help patting himself on the back for making headway on fulfilling his
promise to Angie.

DUKE TRIED TO CALL ANGIE, but got no answer. The next
morning he stopped at the office to run off more flyers to blanket the other end of town. Dinah was heading out to reinterview everyone who lived on Thunder
Road. "Maybe someone will recall seeing a horse trailer
on the road at an early hour on the morning of the robbery," she said.

"Don't forget I'm going to Bozeman at the crack of
dawn tomorrow," Duke told her.

"It's on my calendar. I hope you draw good bulls.
Hey, I'm picking up the T-shirts for the Wild Pony Race
contestants tomorrow. You can reimburse me for your
half when you get back. So, you'd better win."

"I'll do my best. By the way, I followed up on your

suggestion to see Pam Marshall. You were dead-on about Tommy being a pistol."

"I did warn you. Is it going to work out for Angie's son?"

"Maybe. I'll try to find a minute later today to stop at her ranch and give her Pam's phone number. It's ultimately up to the parents to decide."

"I think it's nice how you went out of your way to facilitate things. I hope Angie appreciates you."

He wasn't sure if Dinah was razzing him, so rather than supply added fuel in case she intended to tease him about Angie, Duke mumbled something noncommittal and left the office. He hoped Angie didn't think he was meddling. But he couldn't believe how keyed-up he felt about the possibility of seeing her again.

Driving toward Miles City on the highway, he posted flyers in places where the large font on *Missing* could be seen from a passing vehicle. With luck the word would make some drivers stop to see what or who was missing.

Duke rounded a corner and on the opposite side of the road he saw three or four cars parked with their wheels off the pavement. He slowed to see if someone needed help or if there had been a fender bender.

It turned out to be neither. Passersby were stopped at a roadside stand cobbled together out of weathered wood. The stand sat several yards back off the highway. Duke figured he must have gone by the stand hundreds of times traveling this stretch of county road. But this was the first time he'd noticed it.

On closer inspection he recognized who sat behind the stand selling her wares, and he nearly ran off the road. Angie sat on a folding chair, smiling at customers. Her golden hair hung loose today, and gleamed in the sun. Duke felt his pulse tick up a beat.

He corrected his swerving pickup and drove on until he reached a wide enough spot to turn around. He pulled in as two women got into the first car in line and left.

Duke parked behind a minivan, but there were still two cars in front of it. Nearer now, he could see Luke seated on a blanket slightly to the right of his mother's chair.

More nervous now about what he'd say to Angie, Duke rubbed his palms along the denim covering his thighs. He decided to let Zorro break the ice. Because they wouldn't be far from traffic zipping along the highway, he snapped a leash on his dog. Zorro gave a happy bark and made a beeline for the boy, tugging Duke along.

Luke looked up and saw who was headed toward him. He bounded up shouting, "Deputy Duke and Zorro. Mom, M-Mom, l-look!"

Duke now felt self-conscious because all eyes focused on him. He turned his attention to the energetic child. "Hey, now, call me Duke. Forget the 'deputy' part. It sounds too much like Deputy Dawg," he joked. "That's a cartoon character," he added, when Luke looked puzzled.

"My mom said it's not p-polite for k-kids to only use an adult's first n-name."

"Well, better do as Mom says. But maybe I'll ask her if it's all right."

The boy nodded.

"So what are you doing?" Duke asked.

"R-reading." Luke's expression turned sour. "Mom says r-reading out loud will help me to not s-stutter.

I don't s-stutter when I read to myself. But it's dumb r-reading out loud to nobody."

Duke knelt. Zorro sat with his head in Luke's lap. "Your mom's right on this one, Luke. When you read out loud, you talk slower. It helps if you relax, too." He picked up one of the books. It seemed to be about pirates. "Look at each word, then speak it. That's called snail talk, or turtle reading. Speaking softly is good, too."

"O-k-kay. I'll try. W-will you listen to me?"

"Sure."

The woman at the front of the line waiting to make purchases from Angie, a contemporary of Duke's aunt, wagged a finger at him. "Dylan Adams, you'd better not be here in an official capacity to try and close Miss Angie down. I know the mayor and city council want folks who sell foods or crafts in Roundup to have to buy a special license. They didn't pass that silly law, did they? A group of us protested at the last council meeting." She turned to address the next woman in line. "All residents should call the mayor and tell him requiring a license will cut the number of booths at our yearly fair in half, too."

"Probably more like two-thirds," a third woman added.

Angie held a sack in one hand and in the other a ten-dollar bill the customer had given her. She seemed to be waiting to hear what Duke had to say.

"I haven't heard about any new law, Millie," Duke responded, his eyes assuring Angie, although he addressed the older woman. "Apples," he announced to no one. "I stopped to buy apples."

"That's a relief," Millie exclaimed. "Buying eggs

from Angie here at her stand saves me driving all the way into town." She gathered her purchases, accepted her change and hurried off.

Angie helped her other customers.

Duke shifted to the other knee as he listened to Luke read haltingly about a boy who wished he could be a pirate. Duke helped him sound out hard words, praised him when he got them right, and encouraged him when Luke finished two pages with minimal stuttering.

When her last customer drove away, Angie asked him how many apples he wanted. Her heart squeezed to see him kneel near the blanket, patiently letting her son struggle through reading aloud. She clutched a fist to the center of her chest and blinked back tears. Luke was such a good kid. He longed for friends—longed to be like other kids. She needed more hours in her days. Watching Luke read to the rangy cowboy, Angie felt an ache between her eyebrows. If only Duke Adams was just a deputy and didn't ride in rodeos, she'd be happier.

Angie cleared her throat and called again, "How many apples shall I bag for you, Dylan?"

He glanced up and saw everyone else had gone. "Oh, I don't know. How about a dozen," he said. "Or more, I guess." He didn't need any, but he'd share them at the rodeo in Bozeman tomorrow.

"Did you really stop for apples?" Angie asked as she reached for a sack. "I saw you posting flyers in town yesterday. If someone else told you I'm harboring a black horse, when I get home I swear I'm going to paint white spots on that old gelding."

"No one did that," Duke stressed. He turned to Luke. "You're reading at exactly the right pace. Why don't you read to Zorro while I go pay your mom?"

"Does Zorro know what I'm reading?" Luke gazed in wonder at the soulful-eyed dog.

Duke noticed the kid's speech was perfect. "Zorro's pretty smart," he said. "You only have a few more pages to finish the story. Then you two can toss this stick around." He picked up a short, smooth branch that lay beside the road. "Just make sure you throw toward the woods, not toward the road."

Bobbing his head, the boy bent back over his book.

"It's really good of you to waste part of your busy day listening to Lucas read," Angie said, handing Duke a full sack of apples.

Frowning, Duke pulled out his wallet. He didn't know how much the apples were, but he passed her a twenty. "For the record, I don't consider it time wasted. He does real well reading, and stutters less if someone's there to encourage him and help him slow down."

Now she frowned and slapped change back in his hand. "And how many stuttering boys have you raised, Dylan Adams?"

"One. Me," he drawled softly, but with clarity. "Luke could be my twin at that age. Only, I have a twin, Beau, who never so much as stumbled over a word, let alone a host of them."

Her frown fled and her eyes filled with sympathy. "I'm sorry I snapped. Forgive me. I...uh, no one would know you ever suffered with stuttering to hear you now."

"Yeah." He shifted the sack of apples and tucked his change in a front pocket of his jeans. "It's not something I generally blab about."

"Do you mind if I ask how long, and what you did to

stop the problem? You don't have to answer if it makes you uncomfortable."

Duke gazed into her earnest blue eyes and felt a flicker of answering sympathy. He knew her questions came from a desire to help Luke. "I credit my cousin Ace. He's only two years older than me, but looking back, when we were kids, Ace had a lot of the qualities that make him such a good veterinarian today. He cared, and he was generous with his praise. I'm no expert, Angie. I don't know if every kid who stutters feels like I did."

"Luke started stuttering last year, and it only got worse after Gramps's death."

"I'm not real good at self-analysis," Duke said with a shrug. "With me it lasted about three or four years. I was kind of bashful, and I got teased. I felt out of step."

"What changed that cured you? I don't mean to be nosy, but the speech pathologist led me to believe if stuttering goes on for more than six months, and Luke's has been longer, well, he indicated Luke may stutter his whole life."

Duke shot a glance toward the boy who now laughed and tossed sticks to his dog. "He doesn't stutter all of the time." Duke wished they hadn't started down this path. He believed his stuttering stopped once Ace had helped him toughen up physically, and through bull riding and getting good at it, his self-esteem had shot up.

Angie crossed her arms and she, too, watched her son cavort with the big dog. "I need to work with him more," she muttered. "He's alone too much."

"That brings me to why I really stopped when I saw you out here today. Pam Marshall's twins, Tommy and Bobby, need a third boy to make a team for the Wild

Pony Race. The boys aren't quite a year older than Luke. They are a grade ahead of him."

"I know those boys. Luke sometimes played with Bobby at recess."

Duke set the apples down and got out his wallet again. "Pam gave me her phone number so you can call her about it. Tommy's more rambunctious than Bobby. But I offered to take the boys out to Thunder Ranch and give them pointers on hanging on to a pony long enough for one of them to crawl aboard."

"Is it dangerous?" Angie asked. "The pony someone brought me is so fat and old I can't visualize him running. But he's bitten me, so I don't let Luke feed him."

"I meant to tell you the ponies aren't really wild. Why they call it a wild pony race is because the crowd whoops and hollers, and cowboys get behind the ponies and fan their hats so the ponies will run. The kids are all excited and stumble around trying to hold on to the lead rope while one of their team tries to climb on the pony's back. It takes teamwork, which mostly goes out the window in the carnival atmosphere. That's the area I'd work on with Lucas, Bobby and Tommy, the how of working together."

Angie tucked Pam's phone number in her shirt pocket. "Luke would be ecstatic. I'm the worrywart."

"We have videos at the office of the last few events," Duke said. "For the years Dinah and I have been sponsors. I'm heading out to finish tacking up flyers on our missing stallion. But afterward I'd be glad to stop by the office and grab one of the videos and drop it by here or at your house if you're done here."

"I'd appreciate it. I don't want to make extra work for you, though. Oh, but I'll give you supper in exchange for bringing me the video. I have a chicken cooking in my Crock-Pot, unless you hate chicken," she added quickly, acting as if she ought to snatch back her offer.

Duke laughed. "My family would tell you I haven't met any food I dislike. What time is good?"

"Six. Around there."

They both glanced up as two cars whipped in, stopping in front of Duke's pickup. "I'd better mosey along," he said, retrieving his apples. "I'll see you at six. Do you stay out here that late?"

"Sometimes. I usually stay until I sell out. Why? Are you rethinking coming to the house?"

"No," he said quickly, because couples were getting out of the cars. "You're taking in a fair amount of cash, and we have had all of those recent break-ins. This road is traveled by strangers in the summer who rent fishing cabins along the river."

"I know. People who rent cabins have to eat. Tomorrow I'll have more eggs, and I'm planning to can applesauce, plus jelly I made yesterday will have cooled enough to sell. That and a loaf of bread they buy at the gas-station convenience store, a fisherman has a passable breakfast."

Knowing he didn't have any right to tell her to be careful, Duke nevertheless felt concerned for her safety. Hers and Luke's. "I wish you'd stick to selling stuff in town. A woman alone beside the road is a magnet for danger."

She glanced at him and frowned. "I'm fine here. I open this stand every summer."

"Well, times aren't what they used to be. We didn't used to have break-ins."

"I said I'm fine," she insisted testily.

Duke heard how she bristled. Nevertheless he was of a mind to sit in his pickup until she sold out of everything. But how dumb was that? She'd been on her own quite a while. And that stand didn't spring up overnight.

He walked over to Luke. "I'm taking off. But your mom invited me for supper. You and Zorro can play again then."

"Really? Mom never 'vites anyone to eat with us. Gramps used to. But he's gone to h-heaven to be with God," Luke said, only stumbling over the word *heaven*.

"I'll bet you miss him," Duke said.

"Yep, but he got really sick with 'monia. It hurt him to breathe," Luke said, a knot of wrinkles puckering his forehead.

Duke wished he hadn't said anything to make the boy sad. "I'll bet your mom could use help bagging squash and apples."

"Maybe. Can Zorro stay and play? He can go home with us until you come for supper."

Duke saw the hope glimmer in the boy's gold-flecked eyes. "I would, Luke. I know you'd take good care of him, but I'm afraid he'd try to run after me. As much as he weighs, you might not be able to hold him. We wouldn't want him to get run over."

The boy shook his head.

As Duke loaded the dog into his pickup he saw the two carloads of people had cleaned Angie's stand out of all but a few boxes of her horse cookies. Still hating the thought of leaving her alone out here, he walked back to the stand. "Are the horse treats all you have left to sell?"

"Twenty packs," she said. "A lot of the people who stopped apparently don't own horses. If these don't sell today, I'll take them to Austin's tack shop tomorrow."

"I'll buy them." Duke reached for his wallet again.

"That's generous of you, but where will you use twenty packages of cookies? They don't go stale as fast as people cookies, but even horses like them better fresh."

"I leave tomorrow for the Bozeman Rodeo. I'll pass them around as samples to guys and gals who trailer in their horses. Hey, maybe it'll drum up more business."

Angie took Duke's money and put it in her cash box. Luke, who had slumped along behind the dog, perked up. "You're goin' to another rodeo?" he asked, clearly interested.

"Yes, over this weekend. It's a bit of a drive to Bozeman, so I like to get in a day early to rest up."

"W-will m-my d-dad be there?"

Angie gave a start even though they had heard virtually the same thing from Luke on Duke's first visit to their ranch. She shoved a pile of empty sacks into her son's arms. "Lucas, put those in the Jeep. Right now," she said firmly when it was plain he was going to linger until Duke gave some kind of answer.

Head down, lip out, the boy kicked off through a layer of pine needles.

"Honestly, I don't know why he has this sudden fixation on his father," Angie said with exasperation. "He said my grandfather told him his dad rode in rodeos. Gramps died last November. I would've thought Luke would have forgotten about it by now."

Duke rubbed a finger over his chin. "Other kids may bring it up. There are a lot of rodeo goers in his Sunday-school class."

"None of them would have any idea about his father," she shot back.

"Are you not aware there are rumors floating around town, uh, connecting you to a top-tier bronc rider?"

Angie's jaw dropped. She grabbed up the cash box and wrapped her arms around it. Duke saw color splash her cheeks.

"I didn't know. Obviously my grandfather spoke about my business to more people than just Luke. He should have said Lucas's father would never compete in Montana because he knows I live here. The man wants nothing to do with us." She scraped back her hair with one hand, showing her irritation. "I have no idea where he even is. The last I heard anything about him was before Lucas was born. In any case, he's totally irrelevant," she said with such finality Duke imagined he heard the door slam on any further discussion. However, she also looked kind of sad. So sad, Duke uncharacteristically stepped close and wrapped her in a hug.

Ever so briefly Angie melted against Duke's broad chest. Almost as quickly she looked horrified and pushed away. He dropped his arms at once. Plainly the most flustered, Angie called to Luke, "Get back in the Jeep."

But he loped toward them instead. "I'm coming right now," she said. Brushing past Duke, who had yet to collect his two boxes of horse treats, Angie took a few steps then turned. "The invitation to supper stands, but don't mention the rodeo again around Lucas."

Troubled by her edict, Duke asked, "What should I do if he brings up the subject?"

"Both times he's pumped you it was you who introduced rodeo in the conversation. That triggers his questions. So, just don't…"

All things considered, given how negatively she reacted to one of his two occupations, Duke thought he probably ought to opt out of joining them for supper. But there was the matter of the pony race, and a boy who stuttered who reminded him of himself as a lonely kid. Plus he was flat-out attracted to Angie Barrington. So where did that leave him? With a desire to break down her barriers. For a moment she'd felt soft and feminine in his arms, and she lit fires in him like no woman had before. Like it or not, for just a second, she had hugged him, too.

"Six o'clock," he said, striding past her. "I'll bring the video. My advice concerning it is…you'll probably want to preview it after Lucas goes to bed."

Climbing in the Ford, he set the horse treats on the floor next to the sack of apples he didn't need, and made a U-turn so he could complete his mission of hanging flyers. Why was life so complicated? Why in the devil couldn't he be attracted to a nice woman who loved rodeos?

Chapter Five

At five-thirty Duke entered the sheriff's office and pulled up short. He was surprised to see Dinah at her desk pounding away on her computer. An even bigger surprise, Austin Wright, owner of Wright's Western Wear and Tack Shop, sat on the narrow, uncomfortable bench under the front window. The space was miniscule, and the man sitting there overpowered it with his wide shoulders. Dinah had squeezed in the small bench for people who chanced to walk in at a time she or Duke were tied up on the phone.

She wasn't on the phone, and Duke knew Dinah hated writing her reports on the computer. More often than not she plied him with coffee and doughnuts so he'd type them up for her. So he figured she wanted to look too busy to carry on small talk with Austin.

Duke casually gauged the jut of Dinah's jaw, the way Austin leaned forward with his elbows on his knees and avoided looking at Dinah as he twirled his dove-gray cowboy hat around and around in his hands.

Those two! Duke took a deep breath. Going way back to their troubled high school days for both of them, there hadn't been any love lost between them in a while.

It seemed odd to Duke since both had straightened up and changed course.

"Where have you been all afternoon?" Dinah demanded of Duke.

"All day," he said mildly. "I've been hanging our missing-horse flyers. Is there a problem? You had only to call my cell if you needed me."

"She's huffy because I elected to invade her space for fifteen damn minutes while I waited for you to show up."

"I don't care what you do," Dinah snapped at Austin.

"Whoa, whoa!" Duke spread his hands. "We're all friends here."

Austin got up. "I actually tried to call you, but the ring tone broke off."

"I drove almost to Miles City, could be I was out of range of a cell tower." He pulled out his phone and checked it. "Says I have juice. You're lucky I stopped back at the office. I only came in to pick up one of the videos we shot of last year's Wild Pony Race." That information, Duke aimed at Dinah. Swinging back to Austin, he asked, "What do you need from me, pal?"

"I wondered if I could hitch a ride with you to Bozeman. I did my entry online weeks ago, and today my pickup started acting up. My mechanic says the radiator needs flushing. He can't work on it until the weekend. I could scratch this rodeo, but if I can place in the money it'll help pay for fixing my truck, and other things."

"Hey, anytime," Duke said. "I'll enjoy the company. My plan is to get on the road by six-thirty at the latest. I'll pull up and honk. Do you need a lift to your shop now? Once I grab the video I'll be on my way."

He searched the small bookcase to no avail. "Are those videos in a drawer, Dinah?"

"The TV station is using last year's copy to advertise the upcoming event. Will the two-year-old version do? What do you want it for?" She leaned out of her chair, rummaged in a bottom drawer and tossed a DVD on Duke's desk.

"I saw Angie at her vegetable stand out on the road today and gave her Pam Marshall's phone number," he said, snatching up the disc.

Austin, who had opened the door, glanced back over his shoulder.

"Angie still has concerns centered on safety," Duke explained. "I thought she could watch one of the videos before she contacts Pam. I promised to run it out to her ranch tonight," he said, deliberately not saying he'd been invited out there for supper.

"You're getting pretty chummy with her." Dinah made the observation with a raised eyebrow. "Is she why you shaved and changed out of your deputy duds?"

"Does Angie know the pony race is part of Roundup's rodeo?" Austin asked, saving Duke from answering Dinah. "Judging from remarks she's made during our business dealings, she dislikes most everything about rodeos."

"What business dealings would you be having with Angie?" Dinah probed in a tone doubting the credibility of the man's assertion.

Hustling his friend outside because Duke was already late and he didn't want Dinah and Austin to start World War Three, he called back, "So long, boss. I'll be in touch from Bozeman. Good luck tracking down Midnight while Austin and I are gone."

Dinah got up and followed the men to the door. "What's Angie got against rodeos? It seems the perfect spot for her to hawk her horse treats. If she wore a flashy little outfit she'd sell a ton."

"Some women maybe prefer to be less flashy and more reserved than others," Austin said.

Dinah hooked her thumbs in the service belt she wore that held handcuffs, a nightstick, pepper spray and her Glock. "Says you, who used to only date the flashiest bimbos around, Austin Wright."

"Bye, Dinah," Duke yelled as he all but pushed Austin down the street. "Sure I can't give you a lift to your store?"

"Nah, the walk will do me good." Hunching his shoulders, the other man shoved his hands in his pockets.

"Dinah loves to argue, but she'd be first to come to your aid if you needed a helping hand, Austin."

"Maybe other people. She'd throw my sorry ass in jail in a nanosecond if I ever stepped out of line."

"You've got her wrong. She's really fair." Duke stopped at his pickup, which he'd parked down the street from the office. Zorro sat up and pawed the back window.

"Good luck this weekend in Bozeman, you guys," a sweet voice trilled. The men turned around and Dinah, who had stepped out in the middle of the sidewalk, gave a thumbs-up before she went back into the office.

"See," Duke said, lightly slapping Austin's shoulder.

Austin rolled his eyes. "I'll see you in the a.m. Hey, *is* there something going on between you and Angie?"

Duke straightened. "Going on how? I'm taking her a video of the Wild Pony Race. Why? Do you like her?"

"I do, but not the way you mean," Austin rushed to say, because Duke visibly stiffened. "Unlike you in the Hart clan, Angie had life kinda tough. I identify with underdogs, having been one, and watching my dad flounder for so long."

"Buddy's doing okay now, isn't he?" Duke inquired of Austin about his father, who for a lot of years hadn't been the most upstanding citizen of Roundup.

"Don't know and don't care," Austin shot back. "I'm sure you're aware my sister Cheyenne's living with him again."

"Yeah. I see her and her twin girls now and then with Colt's wife. Cheyenne has cute kids. I was sorry to hear about their dad's passing." Duke shifted uncomfortably. "Well, I'd better get going. See you tomorrow."

Austin waved and trudged on toward his apartment above his store. Duke got in his pickup, greeted Zorro, then tossed the video on the passenger seat and drove off in the opposite direction.

Almost fifteen minutes after six he pulled up outside Angie's back door in a cloud of summer dust. Luke Barrington, who'd been sitting on the back stoop, jumped up and rushed out to meet Duke and Zorro as they left the vehicle.

"My mom said you w-wasn't c-coming," Luke shouted. "I knew you would, 'cause you promised." His eyes shone brightly as he tried to hug the dog and Duke. The boy stuttered only minimally. "What's that?" he asked, seeing the video in Duke's hand.

"It's the reason why I'm late," Duke said, tousling Luke's sandy-colored hair. "It's just something I told your mom I'd pick up from my office. Um, whatever is cooking smells good. Zorro, stay," he added, pointing to an outside rug where Luke had been sitting. "You want to tell your mother I'm here?"

"She already knows," Angie announced, holding the screen door open. "How could I miss hearing all the commotion Luke set up?"

"Sorry I'm late," Duke said as he removed his hat and handed her the video. "I ran into Austin at the office, and we got to talking. I hope it didn't ruin whatever you're cooking."

"The chicken may fall off the bones, but that's the beauty of fixing a one-dish meal in the Crock-Pot. If it cooks too long you call it stew."

"Mom, can Z-Zorro come inside?" Luke asked in a pleading voice.

She lifted her eyes to Duke, and for a moment he got lost in the clear, sky-blue depths. "Uh, whatever works for you," he told Angie. "He's an indoor dog most of the time. But no feeding him under the table," he cautioned Luke.

"Aw."

Angie laughed. "He knows that would have been my edict, too. Here, let me take your hat. Do you need to wash up? The bathroom is down the hall." She pointed and took Duke's hat out of his hands.

It was a narrow hall, Duke discovered, but the bathroom was roomy. In spite of not finding it too feminine or cloying, he suddenly felt jittery. He could probably count on one hand the number of meals he'd eaten with a woman who wasn't part of his family. Not that he worried about his manners. His aunt Sarah had drilled those into her kids and him and Beau at an early age. Keeping up his end of table conversation, that's what concerned Duke. Typically at family gatherings, he sat back and listened and let others talk. At Hart festivities it generally meant a lot of debate if not outright arguing. Duke slicked a wet hand through his hair to keep the dark locks from falling in his face. He rewashed and dried his hands all while trying not to panic. He really was sweet on this woman, and he didn't want to blow his chances of maybe asking her out when he returned from Bozeman, to further explore the pleasure he experienced merely being around her.

"Mom said to t-tell you supper's on the table," Luke hollered through the bathroom door.

Duke yanked it open fast. "I'm coming." Supper being overcooked because he showed up late might be passable. Letting a meal go cold as a result of his dallying would probably not put any points in his column as far as the cook was concerned.

Luke raced to the kitchen table ahead of him and pulled out a chair at the head. "This used to be where our grandpa s-sat," Luke blurted.

"Is it your spot as man of the house now?" Duke asked, smiling down at the boy.

"Uh-uh. I sit across from Mom. You sit here, that way you have to s-say grace."

Duke stopped halfway bent to sit in the proffered chair. He ran a finger around the neck of his T-shirt and shot Angie a helpless look.

"I'll say grace as usual, Luke," she said, "if you'll stop talking and take your chair."

Duke knew, of course, that Angie attended church most Sundays. He attended hit-and-miss with his aunt because he spent a lot of weekends at rodeos. Aunt Sarah asked the blessing at holiday dinners. When they all got together for casual meals or barbecues or for

Super Bowl, they tended to skip blessing the food. Chalk this up to another thing he didn't know about Angie, Duke thought as she bowed her head and thanked God for good health, good food and for his presence at their table as a friend. Duke mulled that over when Angie finished, and Luke piped up to say, "You forgot to say th-th-thank y-you for Z-Z-Zorro being here."

At his name, the dog, who lay by the door, thumped his tail on the floor. They all laughed, and it lightened the mood.

Angie passed him a steaming platter filled with a well-roasted hen, flanked by potatoes, carrots and florets of broccoli all cooked in thick chicken broth.

"Why don't I help Luke take what he wants," Duke suggested, but deferred to Angie.

"Thank you. Give him a drumstick and a spoonful of each vegetable."

The boy made a face and cupped his chin in a palm. "Do I hafta eat broccoli?" he whined.

Angie stared at him. "Need you ask?"

Duke dished out the smallest floret he could find, but said, "Green vegetables build strong muscles. You know all those bigger kids in your class at school— they probably eat second helpings of beans, broccoli and spinach."

The boy watched Duke take a helping of everything before he handed the platter back to Angie. Without further comment, Lucas picked up his fork and the first thing he ate was his broccoli. Duke saw Angie smother a smile.

"Bread? It's homemade herb," she said, taking the top off the butter dish.

"Um, yum." Luke jiggled in his chair and waved his

fork. "It's my fav'rite." Then, looking up at Duke, he asked, "Bread builds muscles, too, r-right?"

"You bet. Home-cooked meals of practically anything taste good and are good for you. This home cooking is a special treat for me."

"Don't you got a mom?" Luke responded, his eyes on Duke.

"Lucas…" His mother put a finger over her lips. She'd heard from Sarah Hart that the Adams twins only had one parent. Not knowing more, she'd hate for her son to inadvertently cause Dylan distress. "Remember, Lucas, Pastor Morrison says some subjects are too personal to bring up in groups where you don't know everyone very well? You just asked a very personal question."

"Oh. B-but we know ev'rybody here."

"It's okay, Luke. I only meant I eat out a lot because I work in town. The food at Sierra Byrne's diner is close to home cooking. I eat there a lot. The people you share a meal with can make eating a more homey experience. So being here with you and your mom is special to me."

Luke beamed. "We like having you here, too, don't we, Mom?" The boy's speech was flawless, but it was plain from the way color rose in Angie's cheeks that he'd embarrassed his mother.

"Glad to oblige," Duke said. "Say, Luke, time's ticking by. If you want to have some time to play catch or fetch with Zorro before it gets dark, you'd better eat up."

The boy did just that. Surprisingly he took one more helping of broccoli and carrots before saying, "May I be 'scused?"

"I made apple pie for dessert," his mother said.

Clearly torn, Luke finally pushed back his chair. "I

want to play with Zorro. Is it okay to save my p-pie till later?"

"All right, but don't go far from the house. The sun will be setting soon."

The boy took off at a run, called to the dog and the pair banged out the back door amid laughter and short, happy barks.

Angie shook her head. "If broccoli gives him any more energy," she lamented, "he'll run me ragged. But, I thank you for getting him to eat a green vegetable. Starting six months or so ago, he began boycotting eating anything green."

Duke laughed. "Probably some kid in school said they were pukey or something. Beau and I went through a period of refusing to drink milk because Owen Harper hated milk and he was the coolest kid in our class. A big, strapping football player, he claimed milk made kids shrimpy. I think we were twelve, an age when boys really start to compare their size and physical prowess with those guys who excel at sports."

"Oh, don't tell me that. Already I've experienced times when Luke's male logic escapes me."

"Did you not have brothers?" Duke asked, curious to learn more about her.

"I'm an only child. You're lucky to have grown up with a brother and a house full of cousins," she said, propping her chin in the palm of a hand.

"I remember Aunt Sarah used to say of her brood that she raised six kids, who each considered themselves an only child. She was counting Beau and me in that. We're all so different. Where did you live as a kid, Angie? Someone said you came from Texas, but I can't place your accent. You don't sound like those of us who grew up in Montana."

"I was born in Tennessee. My dad worked with race horses. Stable work. He cooled out horses that came off the track after exercise runs. Then mom met a race-car driver so the two of us moved with him to Miami. My next stepfather owned a string of shrimp boats in the gulf. At the start of each new marriage, Mom sent me here to stay with her parents. I actually lived in Texas the longest, while she was married to a wildcatter oil-man. I was almost eighteen when she met a vineyard owner and took off for California. We didn't get along, so I balked and stayed in Texas where I worked at a restaurant where tips were big enough to support me. She died of cancer before I got pregnant with her only grandchild. But that's more than enough about my life. Would you like a slice of pie?"

"I'd love it, but I'm stuffed." Duke was sorry she'd stopped short of bringing up the bronc rider that led to her moving in with her granddad. By then, he thought she'd lost her grandmother. As Austin said, Angie had had a tough life.

She rose and began clearing the table.

Duke pitched in to help.

"You don't need to clear plates. If you don't want pie, at least have a cup of coffee. It's ready." She handed him a mug and pointed to where a pot simmered on a cof-feemaker mounted beneath a corner cabinet.

To prolong his visit, Duke poured a full cup. He didn't need caffeine this late the night before he had to get up and leave early on a long drive. On the other hand, the coffee gave him reason to linger.

"Can I pour you a cup? You should eat some of the pie you went to all the trouble to bake."

She waved off his offer. "Pie will keep. Now that Luke is outside, I'll take time to thank you for the video. I'll watch it tonight. I have to go to town tomorrow, so should I drop it off at the sheriff's office?"

Duke felt a jolt because he'd already envisioned coming back after his trip to pick it up as an excuse to see Angie again.

"There's no rush," he finally said once he'd sipped coffee and formulated his thoughts. "I hope you decide to talk to Pam and let the kids meet, too. Dinah thinks they'd make a good team, even though Tommy insists on leading and he likes to win. Don't forget I offered to work with the kids a few times out at Thunder Ranch when I get back."

"When will you return?"

"Late Monday. I'll check with you sometime Tuesday if I may."

"Sure. Is it difficult working as a deputy when you're always shooting off to rodeos?"

"It wasn't until we started having these break-ins," he said, frowning. "Before, Roundup wasn't exactly a hotbed of criminal activity."

"Your aunt is devastated. That stallion is really important to her. Are there any leads as to his where-abouts?"

Duke took another sip of coffee. "Not so far. We sent information about Midnight out to stock barns, auction sites and upcoming rodeos. The thieves may be stuck holding a horse that's too hot to unload easily."

"When I lived at the horse farm in Tennessee, I re-member talk of a ring that stole race horses. They did catch them eventually. They were successful for as long as they were because they dyed the horses in order to sell them. I know I joked about coming home and painting spots on the black gelding if anyone else claimed I had a black horse, and it was later I remembered the case in Tennessee. Could that be a possibility with Midnight?"

"I suppose anything's possible. I wouldn't try to dye a stallion. Especially one born to buck. But greed drives people to do outlandish things. I'll pass along your thoughts to Dinah. Thanks for the tip."

"Part of me hopes you find him soon for Sarah and Ace's sake. Another part of me likes to think of that stallion running free instead of being hauled off to rodeos where he's penned up in fly-infested muck. Or gets stuffed in a narrow chute where he's cinched until it hurts and he's prodded to buck to a stupid buzzer."

Duke's head shot up. "Austin said you dislike rodeos. I assumed your beef was with the riders. Most stock contractors care about their animals. Ace and my dad keep close tabs on the health of our stock. Between rodeos, our horses and bulls are turned out to acres of grass. I've heard old stock contractors say their animals would buck to the buzzer whether or not they wear the belt. Bulls, now, their belt holds a cowbell. The noise of the clanging adds to their frenzy in trying to dislodge it and a rider. But they aren't in pain."

"We'll have to agree to disagree I'm afraid. I've seen too many horses mistreated because they're no longer able to perform."

Setting his empty mug in the sink, Duke collected his hat. "Earl McKinley ran stock for years from Roundup, and now Aunt Sarah does the same. Earl's horses lived to be old and gray. A lot of them retired happily to breed some of the circuit's top buckers. Maybe there are more rules in place now than when your grandfather started his rescue ranch."

"Maybe. I take it you're leaving?"

"I enjoyed the evening, Angie, but I've got an early day and a long drive tomorrow. I need to pack and get some sleep. I'm just glad Austin is going with me, so we'll split driving."

"Austin's entered an event? I thought he quit competing."

"He's not in it for the point standings. He rides when it suits him, hopefully to win some cash. He could be a top contender if he competed more consistently."

"I wonder if he has someone running his shop while he's gone. His store is one of my planned stops in town tomorrow."

"He didn't say when I saw him earlier. You may want to call him. Hey, thanks again for supper. I'll touch base when I get back. I suppose it's too much to ask you to wish me luck in my rides this weekend."

"Do you wear spurs when you ride?"

"No. Neither Beau or I do."

"That makes me happy at least," she said, accompanying him to the door. "Where has Luke gotten off to with your dog?" she muttered, stepping outside to peer around in the fading light.

Duke put his thumb and forefinger to his lips and whistled. Zorro came flying around the side of the house, a red ball still clutched between his teeth. Luke pounded along behind him, hollering, "Hey, Zorro, come back with my ball!"

Dropping to a knee, Duke gently pried the hard rubber ball out of Zorro's mouth. "Here, son," Duke said. "Zorro is trained to come when I whistle. He wasn't stealing your ball."

"Does he gotta go? Can't you s-stay? Didn't we say I c-could read to you tonight?" The boy took the ball, but buried the fingers of his free hand in the fur between the big dog's ears.

"We did, but darn, I'm sorry but I forgot. Apparently you did, too. How about I write a note and post it to my dash, so next time I visit, I'll remember?"

"'Kay." Luke looked dejected, and Duke hated letting him down. He slanted Angie a concerned glance.

Understanding, she stepped off the stoop and slid both hands over Luke's thin shoulders. "I'll put the supper dishes to soak and listen to you read a whole book before bath time, pal. You can pick a book to set aside for Dylan's next visit."

Luke nodded. "I'm gonna pick a fat one, so you've g-gotta stay longer."

Laughing, Duke ruffled the boy's sweaty hair. "It's a deal. Mark it on the calendar. I'll come by next Tuesday afternoon." Straightening, it put him eye to eye with Angie for a protracted moment, until his greater height left him bending nearer to hold on to one last memory of her smile.

"Have a safe trip," she said softly, eyes remaining connected to his as she pulled Luke back against her thighs.

"Thanks." Duke thought it was probably an unprecedented gesture on Angie's part to wish him a safe journey, even if she couldn't bring herself to wish him luck at the rodeo. He tugged hard on the front brim of his hat. "You guys stay safe and take care of each other," he said seriously.

Drawn as he was to her inviting lips, he wished for the easy confidence of Beau and Colt. If they'd been him and felt an urge to kiss Angie, he'd be walking away whistling tonight, taking along the sweet taste of her.

He ended up thinking about kissing her all the way home. He wondered if he would've acted on his urge if Luke hadn't been standing there. Plainly a guy had to be creative if he fell for a woman with kids.

ANGIE AND LUKE STOOD in the yard, watching until Duke's pickup disappeared from view.

"We like Duke a lot, don't we, M-Mom?" The boy leaned back and twisted his face up.

Alarm bells clanged inside Angie's head. Luke might stutter, but he had a brain that worked overtime. Rarely did he make a comment where he included her, or linked their thoughts together that he hadn't planned out ahead of time. If she blurted out a yes, Luke would pounce with a statement leading off with "Then we should..." Then he'd toss out an idea that would be hard to say no to.

"I can see you like him," she said diplomatically. "And his dog. But if you're about to ask me to get you a German shepherd puppy, I'll definitely have to give that a lot more thought. It's time to go in, Luke. You pick a book while I rinse the dishes."

Luke skipped up the steps. "I wasn't going to ask for a puppy. Can you ask Duke out on a d-date?"

Angie gasped. "Lucas Daniel Barrington. Where do you get these notions?"

She slammed the door shut and turned the two locks. With a sigh, she noticed her son wore a hangdog expression. "I'm sorry I sounded cross. It's just…" She threw up her hands. "I thought we said we got along fine after Gramps passed away. Team Barrington, we said we'll be." Angie held up her hand and waited for Luke to give her a high five. He did but it was weak. "What's really wrong, my man? What's eating you?"

"N-nothing. I'll go choose a book." He shuffled off into the other room as she'd seen other kids do when they were burdened by worries. Darn it all, Angie almost wished Dylan Adams had never burst into their lives. She knew Luke had reached an age where he keenly felt the lack of having male influence in his life. She saw how quickly, how readily, her son had set Dylan up in that role.

And truly, in ways that counted the man was gorgeous and nice. He had one major fault. He and his family were into rodeos big-time. No matter how adamantly he swore they coddled their bucking stock, she'd rescued rodeo animals, and had witnessed mistreatment by some rodeo handlers and riders. Oh, why couldn't Dylan Adams have been a full-time deputy? But, after the way she'd been burned by Carter, did she want to risk letting another man—rodeo cowboy or not—in her life?

Chapter Six

Duke pulled up outside Austin Wright's Western Wear and Tack Shop. A small light burned at the back of the shop, but the apartment above lay in darkness. Duke tooted his horn, assuming Austin waited downstairs. Nothing. No one emerged and he didn't see movement anywhere.

Zorro, in the backseat of the pickup along with Duke's duffel bag and riding gear, sat up and whined. Duke had rousted both of them earlier than usual today.

"Austin must have overslept," Duke told his dog. "It'll put us behind, but I need to go get him up. Stay," he said. He shut off the engine and climbed out as faint streaks of gold broke in the east. His long legs carried him up the side stairs two at a time. He knocked hard on the door, knowing if it was him who'd slept through his alarm it'd take an earthquake to wake him. Austin plainly was the same. Duke banged on the door a second time before his bleary-eyed friend cracked open the door. Austin's wavy nut-brown hair gave new meaning to the term *bed head*. Obviously he slept with his head under the pillow.

"Duke? Crap, crap, crap," Austin growled in a raspy voice. "I forgot to set the danged alarm. Can you spare a minute while I pull myself together, or do you need to go? I can call and scratch from my event."

"I'll wait. If you're packed, I'll take your bag down and stow it with mine."

"Uh, no. I'll just toss some clothes in a backpack on the way out the door."

"Tell you what, I'll go gas up my pickup and grab coffee at the station's convenience store. Do you put anything in yours?"

"No, thanks, make it strong and black. I'll be at the curb when you get back."

Nodding, Duke clattered down the stairs.

The gas station on this end of town was in the process of opening as Duke wheeled into the second row of pumps. He hoped they had coffee already brewed. He needed caffeine, and Austin sure as heck did. Jack Turnbull, a teen who worked before and after school at this station of Farley Clark's, greeted Duke almost too cheerfully for the hour.

"Coffee will be ready in a couple of minutes," the boy added. "I'll have a cup poured by the time you pump your gas."

Duke wiggled two fingers as he pulled out his credit card at the pump. "Make it two large cups, Jack."

"Two? You must have had a rough night."

"One's for Austin Wright. He's joining me on the trip to Bozeman."

"You guy's both riding? I thought Austin quit the circuit."

Duke finished at the pump and followed Jack into the store. He paid for the coffee as Jack filled two cups. "Austin's not a regular anymore. His business keeps him too busy."

"He probably hates to give up totally," the boy said. "Hey, good luck to you both. Is your brother or any of your cousins competing?"

"Beau's in bulls. Colt signed up for steer wrestling, plus he's handling stock. Colt's looking good to win the all-around. You have a good day, okay?" Duke opened the door. "Say, you live out past Thunder Ranch, don't you? Did you hear we had another theft? If you open this shift every morning, you must travel that road before daylight. Did you see anyone or anything suspicious or out of the ordinary that morning?"

"Everyone's talking about the robberies. Freaking out. Farley installed new locks at both stations, and we only do credit-card business at the pumps until ten o'clock. But that morning, I only saw Rob Parker pull onto the highway from his lane. He was loaded with baled hay. Traffic was sparse, and no one was pulling a horse trailer."

"Thanks. Keep your eyes peeled, will you?"

"Sure. I probably oughta keep my mouth shut, but, ah…Farley's been telling people Dinah's a lousy sheriff. Gosh, I shouldn't talk about my boss. Don't tell him what I said."

"No worries, Jack. Farley's feelings aren't secret. But, for the record, Dinah's covered all bases. Well, I've gotta run and pick Austin up before our coffee gets cold. Take care."

"You, too." The boy waved as Duke left the store.

Austin lounged against his storefront. A backpack sat at his feet, and he'd tipped his cowboy hat down over his face. Duke wondered if he was asleep standing up, because Austin didn't budge until Duke tapped his horn. Then Austin stretched and slowly moseyed to the curb and crawled into the passenger seat. He seemed to have trouble clipping his seat belt.

"Boy, you need coffee worse than me," Duke said, indicating the cups sitting in holders in the center console.

Austin grunted and mumbled something Duke didn't catch, because Zorro woofed and tried to lick Austin's ear.

"Zorro, lie down and go back to sleep." The shepherd promptly dropped out of sight.

Duke glanced at his friend. In the morning light he looked kind of gray. He didn't immediately reach for his coffee, either, while Duke had already downed half of his. "Did you put in a late night?" Duke asked.

Austin shot him a frown.

"I thought maybe you'd got in a lot of new shirts, pants, boots and stuff for the upcoming rodeo."

"Oh, that. Yeah, I'm displaying some new duds."

"Who's running your shop while we're gone?"

"No one. It costs more to pay part-time help than it does to close for a few days."

"Then I really hope you place in the money. You should have asked Angie to open a few hours a day for you. She said last night she intended to drop off some of her horse treats at your shop today."

"Yeah? Well, I wouldn't ask a favor of her unless I could pay for her time. And I needed to get away for a while. Is that okay? Why the third degree?" Hunched in the far corner of the seat, Austin crossed his arms and settled his hat over his face.

"Jeez. You don't wanna make small talk, fine!" Duke had never noticed before that Austin wasn't a morning person.

By the time he hit Billings and turned onto the interstate, Duke flexed his shoulders and wished for a break. But Austin and Zorro both continued to saw logs.

Approaching Greycliff, Duke nudged Austin. "How about stopping for a burger? Or tacos, we're coming up on a taco stand. Then we can switch drivers."

Austin stirred, but barely picked up the lower edge of his hat. "Not hungry," he mumbled. "Stop here as long as you'd like, but I'm too wiped out to drive."

"Are you sick? Are you going to be able to ride?"

"I'll be fine tomorrow. Jus' let me sleep, please."

Duke didn't answer. He climbed out and slammed the driver's door. He opened the back to let Zorro out and slammed that door, too. *Okay, so that was a tad childish.* He stretched, paced a bit and let Zorro cruise the bushes. The taco stand had outdoor tables set back in the trees. Duke fastened Zorro's leash to a table leg, and he went to order. For all the company Austin was, Duke may as well be traveling alone.

He ordered four tacos with sour cream, and chips and salsa. His pickup bed had a full cover. Under it he'd installed an ice chest and an aluminum side-to-side toolbox. Duke unlocked the tailgate and got out Zorro's bowls, then he grabbed them each a bottle of water. He should offer Austin water. On the other hand why disturb him again?

Duke settled Zorro with food and the timing was good as his order came up. He'd taken one bite of his taco when his cell belted out its raucous tune. "Beau, I'm in Greycliff having lunch," he said, not checking the caller I.D. He assumed his brother had beat him into Bozeman.

"Dylan, it's Angie. I won't bother you if you're eating."

"Wa—…wait," he said, trying to swallow his mouthful of taco. "I was expecting Beau to phone me. Is everything okay? Your ranch wasn't broken into, was it?"

She laughed, and Duke felt the pleasure of the sound all the way to his toes.

"Everything is fine. I didn't need to call, but your aunt Sarah is helping me out this morning and said I should call to let you know I watched the video. Chasing ponies and falling in mud or kicking up dust isn't what I'd call fun, but I was struck by how happy all the kids were. Again, at Sarah's urging, I phoned Pam Marshall. We met at the park, and the boys played on swings and monkey bars. They got along. Luke had such fun. I didn't know Pam makes and sells birdhouses at the fair. She talked me into renting a space to sell my horse treats. I, ah, well… Thank you for hooking us up. That's really why I called, to say thanks from Luke and me. It's all he can talk about."

"Hey, that's great. So, all three boys got along? I admit I had some concerns about Tommy."

"He was a bit bossy, but his brother and Luke didn't object. I, ah, will let you get back to your lunch. Now I can tell Luke I let you know I'd signed him up for the race. He asks every five minutes because he wants to be sure you'll still give them pointers when you return."

"I will. But, Angie, you can phone me anytime. Or Luke can."

She didn't respond and Duke thought they'd lost the connection. "Angie, are you still on the line?"

"Yes. I was trying to think of a circumstance where I may need to reach you again. I hope it's not in any official capacity."

Duke knew he wasn't handling well what he wanted

to get across. "As friends," he finally said. "You know, if you need a man's muscle to help with anything."

"Oh. It's kind of you to offer, but I'm fine. Really, I'll let you go now, Dylan. I hope you don't mind that I call you Dylan," she said in a rush. "It's too weird saying Duke and Luke in the same sentence. I know he thinks it's cool, but…"

"No problem," Duke broke in. "Frankly, 'Dylan' sounds great when you say it."

Again the phone went silent.

"Well, goodbye," Angie finally murmured.

Duke caught himself smiling as he held his dead phone. He liked how Angie had sounded a little breathless. Maybe she felt something for him that went beyond gratitude for his hooking Luke up with a team for the pony race. Duke hoped so. The more they interacted, the more he wanted to spend time with her.

ANGIE HELD THE PHONE LONGER than necessary. There had been times since her grandfather's death that she wished for a man to help do some heavy lifting. Just this morning Miss Sarah brought up that very thing, too. As a rule Angie prided herself on handling things at the rescue ranch alone. However, Miss Sarah struck a nerve when she asked if Angie didn't get lonely. Truly she spent a lot of time by herself or just her and Lucas. But this afternoon she had an appointment to see a woman who was closing her coffee shop on the outskirts of Roundup. The building had everything she needed to expand her horse-treat trade. That would let her hire help, and she would be with people more. But she knew that wasn't the type of loneliness Miss Sarah meant. Even though she and Dylan's aunt had grown closer, and Angie looked up to the older woman, she hesitated mentioning her burgeoning friendship with Miss Sarah's nephew. It was mainly the rodeo involvement she couldn't reconcile—yet here she'd arranged for Luke to enter a rodeo event. Had she just made another big mistake in her life? She hoped not.

LATE AFTERNOON DUKE PULLED into Bozeman and took the route leading to the rodeo grounds. Austin woke up about a mile out of town. He downed the water Duke replaced in the beverage holder. He still didn't say much.

"Did you book a room?" Duke asked. "Beau rented at a cheapie motel. It'd be tight with three bunking there, but we can buy an air mattress somewhere and make do for a couple of nights."

"Thanks, but Baylor Nash called when he saw I'd entered to ride. He arranged for five of us to stay at a B and B. What time do you plan on heading home? I'll bring my gear to the rodeo grounds and hook up with you there."

"Sounds like a plan. Ah, there's Colt's rig." Many rodeo cowboys drove similar pickups, but the ranch logo on the side of Colt's stock carrier stood out. "It looks as if he's already turned the horses into the corrals. Where is the B and B? I'll drop you off."

"We just passed it. But that's okay, don't turn around. I'll get out here and say hi to Colt, then I'll walk back. It'll do me good."

"Suit yourself." Duke stopped. "I can guarantee Beau will vote to eat steak at the Wrangler's Pub tonight, and knock back a couple of beers as we shoot the breeze with other riders. I'll phone you with a time."

Austin hesitated and scrubbed a hand over a face

dark with stubble. "I'll grab a bite at the B and B. I want to look over the horses slated for the bareback event. April was my last rodeo. I need the advantage of studying stats on the field I'll draw from."

"Up to you. I'll undoubtedly see you around. Tomorrow I'm visiting the big stock auction barn to be sure they're on the lookout for Midnight. I ride Friday, and Saturday if I do well. We can skip Sunday's wind-down festivities and hit the road at six again. That is, if you set your alarm," Duke teased.

Austin grinned and for the first time Duke saw a glimpse of the old Austin, who flashed a thumbs-up, then grabbed his bag and hopped out of the cab.

Beau spotted them from wherever he'd been hanging out. He jogged up and yanked open Duke's door. "About time you rolled in, slowpoke. Was that Austin? Where's he going?" Beau slapped Duke on the back in greeting. "Colt's settled the stock, but we're late to go to the pub. I waited to give you a room key."

"Austin opted out of joining us. Point me to the motel."

"I'll hop in and direct you. I parked between two spaces, so I'll pull over and you can park beside me. I'll touch base with Colt if you want to drop your dog and your gear in the room first."

"Sure, but I may make an early night of it. In the morning I'm going to the auction barn. Dinah asked me to check pawn shops that sell Western gear, too."

"Colt is freaked over losing that stallion. Ace thinks he got stolen because Colt proved how good he can buck. He can't wait to get home, as if he has a way of locating Midnight when you and Dinah can't."

"A horse doesn't just vanish. I figure whoever has

him will hide him awhile, then when the furor dies down, they'll sell him for a fraction of his worth. Angie Barrington thought someone might try to disguise him."

"That would be difficult. He's in top form since Ace, Aunt Sarah and Colt fattened him up. I suppose whoever took him could cut his mane and tail." They continued to talk about the horse as Duke stowed his gear. A few minutes later they joined Colt at the pub and more cowboys came up and commiserated over their loss. Duke passed around packs of Angie's horse treats over the course of the evening.

Tired from the drive, he had one beer after his meal to be friendly, then he went back to the motel. He took Zorro for a walk around the arena. Duke considered calling Angie just to hear her voice, but he chickened out and crashed for the night instead.

The next day Beau slept in. Colt joined Duke for breakfast. A lot of old friends came up and asked how they could get some horse treats. Excited for Angie, Duke took their names. He didn't know if she had business cards since she hadn't given him any. Right after breakfast he and Colt drove to the auction barn.

"We have your notices posted where any seller bringing in a horse will see it. No one here takes kindly to horse thieving," the barn owner said.

Taking the owner at his word, the cousins were nevertheless less talkative on the drive back to the rodeo grounds. They parted ways there and Duke hiked to the pens to check out the bulls. For his first ride on Friday he'd drawn a bull called Holy Roller.

"He's big and bad," Beau said, stepping up behind his brother. "He's known for bucking inside the chute."

"Anybody stay on him eight seconds?" Duke asked.

"Not the last two times out. He's in contention for bull of the year."

"Great!" Duke expelled a tightly controlled breath. "Who did you get?"

"Whiskey Sour. He kicks high and comes down stiff-legged. If I can keep from flying off over his head I may be able to ride him out."

"Hey, what's up with Austin?" Beau suddenly asked. "I ran into him at the hot-dog stand and invited him to meet me at five to hoist a brew. He turned me down flat and was acting odd. Distracted."

Duke shook his head. "He slept the whole trip. Outside of him saying he hadn't ridden since April and he needs to land in the money, I don't know what's bugging him. He and Dinah got into it the other evening, too."

"What's new there? Could be he's fighting with his dad again, or maybe with his sister. I asked how Cheyenne is doing, and Austin shrugged is all."

"Are you sweet on Cheyenne?"

Beau frowned. "I'm not interested in her like that, Duke."

"Why not? She's pretty."

"She's got kids and I'm not ready to be a dad. Besides, her husband offed himself. That's a bit too much baggage for me."

"Hmm." Duke thought about Angie and Lucas. "I think you could be a good dad if you cared about the kid or kids and loved their mother." Duke corrected himself to include more than one child because he didn't want Beau digging. But, too late, Beau put two and two together, and Duke had already mentioned Angie too frequently last night.

"Do you have the hots for Angie Barrington?"

Duke scowled at his brother.

"Every guy in the family is falling. The whole time Colt and I were in South Dakota he mooned over missing Leah and the kids. And Ace is gonna be a dad before the year is out. Ain't happenin' to me," Beau declared. "It hurts too bad when a relationship ends. Marriage isn't in my cards," he added, shaking his head. "Not in yours, either, right, Duke?"

"Ri...ght," Duke drawled slowly. But he wasn't at all sure. If he was honest with his brother he might have said he'd thought more about marriage in the past few weeks than he had in his whole entire life.

FRIDAY, THE ATMOSPHERE changed at the rodeo grounds and took on a carnival quality. The air smelled of popcorn and spices as vendors opened up. The grandstands filled, and the beer barns did a thriving business as old friends met up.

Duke, Beau and Colt watched the opening from the sidelines. Colt went off to handle the stock he'd brought. Beau stopped to talk with two of the barrel racers he knew. At two, Duke took Zorro back to the motel and collected his gear for his ride.

Beau turned in a passable score, but it wasn't great. He came to where Duke was clipping on heavy chaps. Duke donned a padded chest plate, but yanked back his hand when Beau took over wrapping it. "Hey, watch it."

"This hand still tender from when you cinched it too tight in Sheridan?"

"Yeah," Duke mumbled. "I brought a thicker glove."

"That's good, but maybe it'd be best if you switched hands."

"I'm not as ambidextrous as you, Beau. This'll be good."

"I think you should wear a helmet with a face mask."

Duke glanced at his brother now helping him buckle on arm guards. "You want me to look like a baseball catcher? You don't wear all this padding."

"Well, it's not cool to wear a helmet, but with this bull it's better than getting your face stomped. You're aiming to rack up points, not trying to impress a lady."

Duke rolled his eyes. "I hate wearing a mouth guard, but if Holy Roller is a chute slammer, he could break my jaw."

Beau agreed.

The big bull was indeed a chute slammer. Handlers yanked Duke up out of the chute four times before the snorting animal quit fighting enough for his rider to lock on and get a good seat. The instant the chute opened Holy Roller crashed back into the side of the chute, catching Duke's left leg. He shot his right arm up calling a fair ride so as not to lose precious seconds. It indicated to a cheering crowd that he wasn't injured.

The bull bucked and kicked, attempting to dislodge Duke and the clanging bell cinched to his belly. He whirled and spun in dizzying circles, snapping Duke's head forward and back. Clinging with his knees and heels, Duke slid to one side. He counted off seconds in his addled brain.

At last the horn blew and the bullfighters moved in. Duke released his grip on the rope and kicked off the still-crazed bull. Holy Roller whipped around, forcing Duke to race toward the nearest fence in a galloping hobble. A roar of approval went up from the bleachers as Beau and Colt pulled Duke up. The bull escaped the clowns and made one last bellow and tried to butt Duke's backside.

"Wow, you are one lucky dude that bull's horns turn down instead of up and out," Colt said, breathing hard as he gave his cousin a congratulatory backslap.

"You'll earn extra points for staying on past the buzzer on such a rough ride. How's the leg?" Beau asked, watching Duke rub his left knee.

"It's not broke. Mostly my knee got whacked. It'll be black-and-blue by morning."

"Think you can ride tomorrow?" A guy with a clipboard stepped out from behind Colt. "If your time holds up, and since Dan Ralston just got throwed at first bounce, it looks as if you get your pick of bulls for tomorrow."

"How about Hornet? He gave me a good ride a couple of months ago."

"You got it. I'll turn in your choice. Better ice that leg, son."

"Guess so. I brought a few blue ice packs. How did Austin do? I missed watching his bareback event."

"He did really well. If he turns in an equivalent ride tomorrow, he'll win some cash. As will you, my man," Colt said, sounding pleased.

That was the best thing about being a rodeo family, Duke thought as he limped to the room. They could be in fierce competition, but they all rooted for one another in the end.

Beau caught up to him outside the motel. "My time wasn't good enough to let me ride tomorrow. I'm going to pull out at first light and catch the rodeo in Great Falls."

"Will you make it back for ours in Roundup?"

"Only if I haul ass. Don't lecture, Duke. I'm teasing. You know I wouldn't miss the hometown gig. But if I hope to match you in cash, I've gotta ride in twice the rodeos as you."

"That's bogus, Beau. I've watched you ride bulls for years. You have a better style and, in general, ride smoother than me."

Beau hooted with laughter. "You can say that with a straight face—you who are only points away from the national finals?"

Duke shucked the rest of his gear and stooped to pet Zorro before he dropped down on his bed and took the ice pack Beau dug out of the cooler. "Tell me why you win when we aren't competing against each other?"

Beau looked startled. "I don't know. Maybe you get better bulls."

"Sure...like I did today? Oh, forget it. I don't want to argue," Duke said.

"We can't both be top dog. Colt's winning well. Thunder Ranch is looking good."

"Yeah. I've been thinking if I win at Nationals, Aunt Sarah and Ace can make a splash with it on Thunder Ranch's website. You know, top stock and top contenders."

"You bet," Beau said, grinning as he handed his brother the ice pack.

SATURDAY DAWNED. DUKE'S LEG felt somewhat better, but as he'd expected, it was discolored. He moved his gear to his pickup so Beau could check out and take off for Great Falls. The second day of a rodeo, fans who held tickets to all the events tended to be hardened rodeo buffs. The best riders rode on day two, adding to the excitement and the pressure.

Colt found Duke at noon. "Listen, coz, my stock are done competing before your ride. I'm finished, and Austin rides next. If you don't care, I'm gonna leave. Austin said he'll help me drive. If you don't hang around until morning, you'll catch up to us. Pulling a trailer filled with stock slows me down."

Duke thought about telling Colt good luck on getting help driving from Austin, but that might sound like sour grapes. "You go on ahead. I may find a room and spend the night. I should have kept the one Beau had, but I let it go since he was paying. I like to shower after a ride and rest a bit. Tell Dinah we came up dry on leads here on our thieves."

"Will do. Have a good ride and take care driving home. We're all going to be working hard the next couple of weeks getting ready for our fair and rodeo."

"That reminds me. I promised to train a team of little guys for the Wild Pony Race. Can you spare me a corral for a few days, and scare up a couple of ponies?"

"Sure. I can't wait till Davey is old enough to enter, but Leah signed Jill up. She's tough like her mother." Duke smiled as Colt's obvious pride in his stepkids puffed up his chest. But then Colt's own smile dimmed. "I just wish I had had the brains to be there for Evan when he was younger."

Duke knew Colt would always regret not playing a part in his own son's life. "Have you seen Evan lately?"

"I managed to see one of his baseball games, but I hope to see more. He's quite a kid." Colt shook his head, then asked, "Say, whose kids are you training for the pony race? That's not something you generally do."

"The Marshall twins, and Luke Barrington."

"Interesting trio—you should have your hands full with them. Okay, Duke. See you back at the ranch."

Duke leaned on the fence and watched Austin ride to the money. He thought about Colt's remarks and how much more settled he was since he'd married Leah and become a stepfather. Colt used to be a hellion. Dinah, too. Amazing how people changed. For Colt it took meeting the right woman. For Dinah, she got interested in the law.

Before Duke knew it, it was time for his ride. He suited up and today he didn't wear a helmet. Fans expected a champion to pump a fist in the air and ride waving his cowboy hat, so he would put on a show.

Unfortunately, Hornet had a few tricks he hadn't exhibited the last time Duke rode him. He became a nose-to-the-ground twister.

Twice Duke faltered. He missed staying on to the buzzer by the skin of his teeth. Thanks to the clowns, he didn't get gored as he rolled away in the dirt.

Bucking horses tended to buck to the buzzer, then stopped. Bulls bucked until they dislodged their rider, then tried to kill him. Duke's rope hand got banged again, and he smacked his bruised leg, as well. Thankfully his times held up, and he earned some nice money. He'd just collected his winnings and limped with Zorro to a motel where he booked a room when Beau called.

"I watched your ride on TV, hotshot. Sloppy, sloppy, sloppy is the best I can say. You're danged lucky you pulled out the points."

"Yeah, yeah. Let's see you turn in a better ride in Great Falls." Irritated because he thought he'd done pretty well, Duke clicked off, tossed the phone aside and stepped into the shower. Coming out dripping, he decided to head home after all instead of staying the night. He dressed, paid his bill and loaded up. He'd never admit it wasn't Beau's needling that made him want to get home, as much as a strong desire to see Angie again. Visions of her hovered at the back of his mind, and had him ticking off mile posts in anticipation.

Chapter Seven

He reached Roundup in time for breakfast and saw the work already underway for the upcoming fair and rodeo. The fair started a week before the rodeo, and both ended the same Sunday.

Banners painted with bucking horses and the dates for the rodeo were strung from light post to light post all down the main street. Store windows had been washed and many were decked out in Old West themes. Crews had begun nailing together rows of booths that would soon be filled with goodies and crafts waiting to be sold.

Duke had noticed along the pass that some tree leaves were already changing color. Few cowboys or ranchers looked forward to Montana winters. Duke was no exception and he hated to think about summer giving way to fall. But the fair and rodeo always meant that if they were lucky they might get a month to six weeks more of good weather before snow started to fly.

He was tempted to veer off onto the side road that would take him to Angie's ranch. But it was early and he hadn't established times to take the kids to Thunder Ranch for wild-pony instruction, so instead, he contacted Dinah. "I'm pulling up in front of the Number 1 Diner, any chance you care to meet me for breakfast?"

"I'm at the ranch. Mom says she'll feed you if you come on out here, champ. Colt told us about your rough ride. Mom wants to see for herself that you're all right."

"Colt's a blabbermouth. But, yeah, I'll be there in fifteen minutes." His aunt Sarah loved to cook. Duke knew she'd feed him well.

He and Zorro walked right in without knocking. Dinah, his aunt, and Leah and her two kids were in the kitchen. Jill and Davey were still shy around their uncle Duke. Zorro loved kids. He barged right up to the table where the kids played with a farm set. Davey squealed and drew back from the dog's wet, black snout.

"Zorro, mind your manners," Duke ordered. "Sit and shake hands with Jill." The dog sat and lifted a paw to Jill who was nearest. Both kids giggled. "He won't hurt you," Duke said, dropping to their level to facilitate the meeting. When he went to stand again, his sore leg let him down and he stumbled backward into the counter where his aunt had dished out his piping hot breakfast.

"Whoa there!" Dinah's quick reaction saved him from falling over.

"I'm okay," he said, mostly to assure Sarah, who didn't need any more to worry about. "I drove straight through the night. I thought I might catch Colt and Austin, but they had quite a head start."

"Colt pulled in around 2:00 a.m." Sarah handed Duke utensils. "I sleep light since the last break-in. Dinah's been telling me how quiet it's been in the area since they broke in here a second time."

"Quiet is good." Duke scooped scrambled eggs onto his toast. "Did Colt tell you we visited several pawn shops and secondhand stores? Everyone had our lists of stolen goods and said they're keeping an eye out."

Sarah leaned on the counter and rubbed her forehead. "I'm afraid Midnight is gone for good."

Dinah put an arm around her mother. "I tell you he will turn up. I feel it in my bones."

Duke washed down his toast with coffee. "I think so, too, Aunt Sarah. We got information out across Montana and even to neighboring states fast. My guess is when they figure out they can't sell him for big bucks, they'll let him go cheap to keep from feeding him. We just need to stay vigilant."

Dinah sat again. "I talked to some auctioneers and others in the business of buying and selling horses about Angie telling you a thief might attempt some kind of disguise. Midnight is such a one-of-a-kind stallion, the consensus was it'd be hard to change his appearance enough to not arouse suspicion."

Duke finished eating. He and Dinah left the house together. "I need a word with Colt," he said. "I'll stop by my apartment then meet you at the office. I'm worried about the ranches when folks come to town for the fair or rodeo."

"Me, too," Dinah said. "I've been thinking about that. We need to work out a plan to patrol. I'll ask the mayor if he'll authorize you some extra hours, Duke."

"If not, I'll work for free. It galls me that those guys are decimating our territory. You know the rest of the family will make sweeps, too."

"Ace said the same thing. But he's swamped now, and it's my responsibility."

"I still think they'll slip up and we'll nab them." Duke hooked an arm around her neck, shaking her a little to buck her up.

She did smile, and Duke went in search of Colt.

"Hiya," Colt greeted his cousin. Early as it was, he already had mucked out half the stalls. "Ace tells me the small corral where he sometimes quarantines a horse is available for you. I can have two ponies here by tomorrow."

"Thanks. That's what I wanted to check on before I got the kids all excited. I'll contact Angie and Pam Marshall this afternoon."

"Oh, I almost forgot. Mom said have the kids bring swimsuits. After your lesson they can have a snack with our kids, and all of them can swim awhile. I know the boys are older than Davey and Jill, but it'll be good for them to have someone to play with."

"I saw Leah and Austin's sister at the park with all the kids one day."

"Cheyenne sometimes brings Sadie and Sammie out here, too. Our swimming pool has been getting a lot of kid action lately. Luke and the Marshall twins will have a ball."

Duke thanked his cousin for arranging everything then left the ranch and headed to Angie's. He continued to worry that her place was too secluded. But maybe she liked having space to herself. Yet he couldn't help but wonder how, or if, a man might fit into Angie's life.

She and Luke were gathering eggs at the henhouse as Duke drove in. Luke spotted him first and raced toward his pickup, waving his arms. Duke could tell Angie tried to stop the boy even as she juggled an egg basket.

Duke stopped short of the house so Luke wouldn't plow right into his pickup. He got out, released Zorro, and the boy and dog wrestled around in a cacophony of noisy barks and boyish laughter.

"Honestly, I'm sorry he's such an introvert," Angie

said, rolling her eyes as Duke approached and relieved her of the basket. "What brings you out so early?"

"Helping you gather eggs. I lost you your egg partner."

"I'm almost finished. Did you have a good trip? I notice you're limping. Did you get hurt again?"

Duke hesitated talking about his bull ride, knowing her feelings on the subject. "I bumped my leg is all. I came by here for two reasons. Three, really. I missed you and wanted to see you again," Duke said first, surprising himself for stating his feelings so boldly. "Also," he rushed on, "I gave out samples of your horse cookies. I can't tell you how many horse owners asked where they could buy more. I took down a few names and addresses." He pulled out his wallet and gave her folded slips of paper. "You need business cards. A lot of guys asked why your address isn't on the package label."

"Mitch from the print shop, who does my labels, said since I make the product here where I live alone, maybe it wasn't a good idea to list my address."

"Makes sense. Have you considered selling online? It's easier to be removed from customers. I'd be glad to build a website and show you a few marketing possibilities. I don't know how much you want your business to expand."

"That's generous of you." Her eyes sparkled. "While you were gone I rented Ruby Winston's coffee shop. She's quitting and her shop is perfect for my needs. There's a large kitchen, and glass cases in the eating area that will take the place of my roadside stand. Selling online sounds like another option."

"I'm glad you're leaving the roadside stand. I've seen

some online businesses really take off. I can help you set up."

She nodded. Putting three more eggs in the basket, she took it back from Duke and walked toward the house. "You...uh...mentioned having three things you came for," she said, clearing her throat and looking self-conscious.

"The other is training the boys for the pony race. Colt has a corral I can use, and he's got two ponies all lined up. Oh, and Aunt Sarah invited the boys to stay for snacks afterward. Colt suggested they bring swimsuits and they can play on the jungle gym, and then swim with his and Leah's two kids. Does Luke know how to swim?"

She shook her head. "He does have a suit he wears to run through our sprinkler on hot days."

"If you can get away around eleven tomorrow, come along. Colt's kids are younger than Tommy, Bobby and Luke. The more eyes around a pool the better."

"I'd love to, but I volunteered to help put together fair booths, and my shift is eleven to twelve tomorrow and Thursday."

"So, throw your suit and a towel in the car and drive out to Thunder Ranch when your shift ends. I plan to work with the boys for about forty-five minutes. If I include driving time, the session will wind down at twelve-fifteen or twelve-thirty."

Her gaze cut to where Luke and Zorro chased after a ball. "Luke asked every day when you were getting back. He's so excited about the Wild Pony Race he can hardly stand it. He's not the most coordinated kid, Dylan. I'm sure you won't expect perfection, but..." She broke off, imploring him with big eyes.

Duke was moved to lean over the egg basket, tilt up her chin and brush a kiss over her softly parted lips. "No kid was ever more awkward than me, Angie," he said earnestly. "I felt a kinship with Luke when we met. I don't want to worry you. Why I'm training the kids is for Luke. Ace helped me come out of my shell. I hope being on this team will boost Luke's confidence."

"You kissed me," Angie whispered, her whole body trembling.

"I did. Should I apologize?"

"Ah...no." She stepped back. "It's... I... What if Luke had seen?" she mumbled. "I don't have men in my life, Dylan."

He rubbed his whiskery cheek, thinking he should have cleaned up before kissing her. "You have me."

"I...can't."

"Why?"

"It's the rodeo, Dylan. It's the way handlers, contractors and riders mistreat animals. I have grave reservations about letting Lucas get involved in even this so-called simple kids event. And you obviously love everything about the rodeo."

"I do. I think you're not giving it a chance because of problems you had with Luke's father. That's not fair, Angie."

"Stop it. You don't know what you're talking about. I'm trying to let Luke be in that pony race. I think you'd better go before I change my mind." She clutched the egg basket and looked away.

"All right," he said stiffly. "You have to do what you think is best." He whistled for Zorro, told Luke goodbye and backed his pickup down the lane.

He shoved a disk in his CD player, but didn't feel like

listening to another brokenhearted cowboy song. He'd hoped there'd be an opportunity for him to ask Angie out to dinner and a dance. Now that seemed highly unlikely. He guessed he'd know when he saw Pam Marshall if he'd be forced to disappoint the kids.

SHE DIDN'T END UP PULLING Luke out of the event. So the next day Duke picked up the Marshall twins before going to the Barrington ranch. It was calculated to avoid further argument with Angie. Duke figured he needed time to prove to her that he and his cousins were good stewards of the animals they worked with. During the night he discovered he still felt she was worth him making an effort to change her mind about rodeos and rodeo cowboys.

Taking three boys in his pickup meant he had to wipe doggie paw prints from the back leather seat before digging out three sets of seat belts. It was rare for him to transport anyone but Zorro. If he made inroads and Angie agreed to go out with him, he'd have to do more to the Ford than wipe down the seats.

Luke sat fidgeting on his back stoop and bounded to his feet the minute Duke entered the lane. He saw Luke run into the house and race back out with his mother following at a more circumspect pace. She carried his backpack. "He's wired in high voltage," she told Duke as he left the cab and opened the back door for Luke to crawl in.

"I packed sunscreen, his bathing trunks and a towel," she said, as if none of their argument had happened.

"Right," Duke said, setting the pack at Luke's feet. "Buckle up, boys."

He noticed Luke was stuttering through a greeting

to Tommy and Bobby and saw Tommy, who'd claimed the spot by the window, had turned away. Duke would like to caution Luke to speak slower, but he didn't want to embarrass him.

"Miss Sarah phoned to invite me out to the ranch, so I'll be there after my shift," she said, plainly feeling him out.

"Oh, okay. You can park near the house," he told her.

"I keep vacillating about going," she said, riffling a hand through her hair.

"I'm sure Aunt Sarah will be disappointed if you don't show up." To say nothing of himself, because he was warming to the idea again.

"Oh, I suppose. Will she and Leah swim? I wear a swimsuit so seldom. I... Oh, you don't care about a self-conscious woman."

Duke removed and resettled his hat, slanting it over his eyes. His heart skipped imagining Angie in a skimpy bathing suit. Closing the back pickup door, he rubbed a knuckle over his jaw. "I'd be a fool to respond to that comment, Angie. See you later." He climbed in the front, tossed his hat on the console and didn't look back as he left her standing in the lane. But it took all of his control to not look.

At Thunder Ranch the boys piled out and ran to the corral where the ponies trotted around.

Duke lined up the boys and explained what he expected each to do. Because Tommy had long ago claimed the right to be the team member to mount the pony, that left the two smaller boys to nab the rope and keep the pony from crossing the line prior to Tommy getting a leg over the animal's back.

Following three or four failed attempts, Tommy,

red-faced and upset, lit into Bobby and Luke, blaming them for not hanging on tight enough to the rope. Duke showed them how to snag the rope and wrap it once around their hips to give their heels more traction in the dust that littered the corral.

"Tommy, they are doing their best," he said. "Maybe it's time for a soda break." Duke went to the back of his pickup and got four sodas out of the ice chest. All of them rolled the cold cans across sweaty foreheads before popping them open. It pleased Duke to realize Luke hadn't stuttered in quite a while. And the kid seemed to really get a kick out of wallowing in the dirt.

Colt entered an adjacent corral leading a horse Duke recognized as a newly acquired gelding. Colt slipped a hackamore over the gelding's head and the horse tore loose, bucking all the way around the corral.

The boys got up from where they were sitting and as one moved toward Colt.

"Hold on, boys," Duke called. "If you get too close you'll spook the horse worse than he is. I'll let down the Ford's tailgate. You all can sit there and watch Colt until you finish your sodas."

Duke was glad for the break. Tommy Marshall was proving to be a bigger pain in the butt than he'd expected. In truth, the smallest boy had the best chance of leaping on the pony because bigger kids did better holding the ponies back. But that wasn't going to happen. Tommy had struck the deal to be the one to ride the pony, and he wasn't budging.

Duke's dad drove up in one of the ranch hay haulers seconds after Colt climbed on the gelding, and the boys started to whoop.

Joshua moseyed toward them, and Duke met him halfway.

"What are you doing with all the kids?"

"Not making as much headway as I'd hoped giving them pointers on surviving the Wild Pony Race," Duke said, laughing. The men leaned arms atop the pony corral.

"I heard one of those Chilean bulls slammed you around in Bozeman," Josh said.

"He was tough, but I'm okay. Hey, Beau mentioned Aunt Sarah may phase out the remaining beef cattle and the bucking bulls. Are you okay with that?"

"The work is getting old. Or else I am," Josh grumbled. "I haven't been as happy since we quit running a real herd. I've been a cattleman all my life."

"You aren't old enough to retire, Pop. What'll you do with your life?"

Josh didn't answer, but stared at the distant hills, seeming dispirited. Duke thought about how his own spirits lifted when he saw Angie, or when he imagined seeing her.

"I hear somebody's teaching line dancing every Wednesday night at the Open Range Saloon. Maybe you ought to go. Get out some and improve your social life."

"Are you kidding? Don't I always say, 'find what you're not good at, and keep not doing it'? That's how I'd be if I tried to line dance…not good at it."

Breaking off with a growl, Josh hopped back in his vehicle and drove off in a cloud of dust. Duke pondered how flustered his dad had seemed. He shouldn't have tried to tease his father. They'd never had that kind of a relationship, sad to say.

In the corral, Colt slid off the tired gelding and led

him out the far gate to turn him into a field with other bucking stock.

"We're hot," Tommy Marshall complained. "Can we go swim now, and do this another day when it's cooler?"

Duke checked his watch and found they had been here over an hour. "Maybe we've done enough for your first day."

They drove to the house and Duke was heartened to see Angie's vehicle. He herded the kids and dog around back.

Leah, his aunt and Angie were already at the pool. Leah played with her children in the shallow end. Duke didn't want to stare at Angie in her suit. It was modest as suits went, but she filled it out in all the right places, and he wondered how those curves would feel under his roving hands. Duke swallowed at the thought.

"They're all little kids," Tommy whined, jarring Duke out of his daydream. "I like doing cannonballs."

"No cannonballs," Duke snapped, his patience with Tommy Marshall near its end. "This isn't a swim party, it's meant to cool everyone down."

"How did it go?" Angie asked, squinting up at Duke after Sarah ushered the boys into the house to change into their trunks.

"Chaotic, but I expected that for the first go-down."

"You look frazzled. And you're favoring your injured hand again." She reached out and touched his knuckle.

Duke reacted at once to her soft touch. Then he noticed Leah watching them. "I probably tugged too hard on the rope while trying to show the boys how to hang on to the pony. I'd better go change into my suit, or the wild kids will be out here jumping in, splashing everyone."

He walked off. Angie dropped her sunglasses over her eyes, but not before she imagined how Dylan's broad shoulders and slim hips would look in swim trunks. And she shouldn't be having those kinds of thoughts.

"Gotta love the slow hip-roll of a cowboy's walk," Leah remarked.

Angie hadn't realized she was being scrutinized. "I don't deny cowboys are easy on the eyes."

"Hmm. That implies they fall short in other areas."

The three boys burst out the house door, trailed by Sarah, who juggled a tray filled with glasses and a pitcher of lemonade. Pretending she hadn't heard Leah's comment, Angie jumped up and ran to assist Sarah.

"Oh, thanks, Angie. I have the tray, but could you go into the kitchen and bring out the cookies? Lisa Marie baked three types. There should be a kind to suit everybody."

Angie hurried into the house and nearly bowled Duke over. Her hands landed flat against his naked chest, and she felt the barest prickle from his chest hair. Unable to stop her response, she flexed her fingers once then snatched back her hands. "Sorry. Sarah sent me after cookies. I assumed the door opened straight into the kitchen."

"No, it's down the hall on your left. Here, let me show you."

"Oh, wow, it's a full platter. A lot of cookies for a small group. I'll need to monitor the boys or they'll go home with sugar highs or bellyaches."

"That looks heavy. Let me carry it for you," Duke said.

Angie didn't readily release the platter she was using as a shield from the man's dark and roaming eyes. "I…

ah...thought a lot last night about what you said about selling my horse treats over the internet. It sounds great, but I don't own a computer and I'm not sure I should invest in one just yet."

Duke lengthened his stride to stay even with her, and didn't mind at all that their bare arms brushed as he shoved open the door for her to go out first. "I have an extra laptop. I can set up a trial site before I bring it over. There are free programs for small business owners that I can download. You don't have to ship any product until the money is in your bank. Or you can arrange for a PO box at the post office and fill orders that way for people who prefer to pay by check."

"I know a little about that," Angie said.

"What are you two ordering?" Sarah asked, taking her eyes off the boys.

"Angie is expanding her horse-cookie trade. I took samples to Bozeman and a lot of the guys who travel to rodeos wanted to know how to buy more. I offered to help her set up a website."

Leah glanced up. "Cheyenne's considering selling her jewelry that way, too. I wish I had talent, or some way to earn extra money."

Sarah, who sat with her legs dangling over the pool's edge, patted Leah's hand. "I've never met anyone as organized as you or as good keeping accounts straight. You have a marketable skill. Get Cheyenne and Angie to hire you as their bookkeeper." Sarah turned to Angie. "If you run a business, you don't have time to do everything. Leah saved us time and money almost the minute she took over the ranch accounts."

"Miss Sarah, I've no doubt you're right, but I'm renting Ruby Winston's coffee shop, so I'm not sure I can afford Leah until I see if my business grows."

Duke was happy to hear her say that. If Leah took over Angie's accounts, she'd be the one to set Angie up on the computer. He was picturing evenings where the two of them cozied up and worked together.

"It's a thought for the future," Leah said. "Hey, there's Colt. Jill, Davey, come on and dry off. Grab one cookie each and we'll trek home and leave the pool to the bigger kids."

"Yay," Tommy yelled. He didn't act contrite, either, when Duke scolded him and said he should apologize to Jill and Davey. The boy mumbled something indiscernible, and Duke choked off a sigh. Tommy was just a kid. Getting angry with him wouldn't teach him manners.

Duke eased into the pool. He stayed toward the middle where he could get to Tommy doing cannonballs at the deep end if need be, or Lucas kicking his feet on the steps in the shallow part, or Bobby dog-paddling somewhere in between. "Luke, do you want to learn to do what Bobby's doing?" Duke asked quietly.

"It looks h-hard," he stuttered.

"Only if you let it frighten you. Moving your feet and hands keeps you floating on top of the water." Duke held out his hands palms up and coaxed Luke to lie across them. "I have you and I won't let you slip under. Practice kicking your feet up and down and moving your hands the way Zorro moves his feet. That's why it's called dog-paddling."

"I didn't know dogs liked to swim."

"Some do. On hot days they need to cool off the same way people do."

Angie sat at the table with Sarah. They chatted a bit

about a range of topics, but Angie's gaze followed Duke in his patient effort to teach her son to paddle and enjoy the pool like the other boys were doing.

"My nephew is a good man," Sarah remarked suddenly. It was plain, however, that she noted something in the way Angie kept dropping the thread of their conversation.

Angie flushed.

Sarah refreshed their glasses with more lemonade. "Duke probably hasn't told you, but he was once a lot like your Luke. Quiet. Shy. Not really timid, but far from gregarious like his twin and his cousins. He had a speech problem, too."

"He credits Ace with helping him gain self-confidence." Angie frowned slightly. "To see Dylan today, no one would believe self-confidence was ever a problem."

"I love hearing you say that. Ace got him interested in bull riding. Mercy, he's come so far. My brother did his best, Lord love him. He raised two boys alone in a day and age when men rarely did that. I don't mind stepping up and taking credit for Duke's sensitivity, though." She winked. "You know…a woman could do worse than snagging him for a husband."

Angie realized Sarah meant her. "Oh, Miss Sarah, there's nothing of that sort between… We, uh, I…" Angie broke off and felt her cheeks flame as she remembered dwelling on a kiss he'd delivered, and she'd gotten huffy to hide her real reaction of liking the kiss.

"I'm not trying to meddle," Sarah murmured. "Heavens, I'd be the last person to play matchmaker. Two of my sons fell in love right under my nose and I didn't see either marriage in the offing ahead of time."

Angie dropped her sunglasses over her eyes. "I had

a bad experience with love, Miss Sarah. I'm not sure... How will I know?"

Sarah patted Angie's knee. "Just keep an open heart and mind."

Angie mulled that over as she listened to her son's excited babble and watched Dylan's patience with him. Maybe she could open her heart.

Luke dog-paddled halfway across the pool before he realized he was doing it on his own. He faltered, sank and came up choking. Duke snatched him up, patted his back and stood him up out of the water, wrapping him in his towel. "That's probably enough for one day," Duke said. "Tommy, Bobby, time to go. I promised your mom I'd have you home by three."

"Oh, Luke, we need to go, too." Angie wasn't wet, so she stepped into jeans, boots and stuffed her blouse in a tote she'd brought.

"May I ride home in my suit?" Luke took a cookie, then looked to her for permission.

"If you sit on your towel. Hot as it is, you'll dry quickly. Thank Dylan and Miss Sarah," she prompted.

Luke parroted a thank-you. Bobby chimed in, with Tommy a bit slower. "I want to go in and change," he announced. His brother concurred through a mouthful of cookie.

"I want to change, too." Duke paused next to Angie. "I told the boys we'd try another lesson Thursday, only earlier to miss the heat of the day. Is Luke up by nine?"

Angie nodded, but continued to steer Luke toward her vehicle.

Duke couldn't resist watching her walk away.

As Luke buckled in and wiped cookie from his face, he bounced a little in his seat. "Mom, I had the funnest time ever. But can we have broccoli or spinach tonight? Bobby and me need to get heavier so we can hang on to the pony. Remember when Duke came to supper? He said green vegetables build muscles."

Praise the Lord, Angie thought. "We can manage a green veggie," she said soberly. "So you liked all of the day, including chasing after the pony?"

Luke laughed and got louder and louder as he relayed incidents that tickled him. Angie didn't remind him to lower his volume, it was so good to see him happy, and he hadn't stuttered once. She had Dylan Adams to thank for that. She mulled over tidbits Miss Sarah had shared about his life. And yes, the man would be good husband material if his acquired self-confidence had come from mucking stalls, or stacking hay bales instead of from tying a cowbell around a bull and riding the poor animal into a frenzy.

Duke's aunt collected the pitcher and glasses. "Angie is the sweetest thing, and she's a great mom. She'll make some lucky man a fine wife one day."

Duke shot his aunt a hooded glance and almost dropped the plate of cookies he'd picked up. Sarah held up a hand. "It was only an observation. You know I'm no matchmaker."

Duke reflected on her casual, yet calculated comments as he drove the Marshall boys home. His aunt could be sneaky. But maybe he should let her know he wouldn't object if she did a little matchmaking.

Chapter Eight

A call at 3:00 a.m. sent Duke and Dinah to a dairy farm off the upper river road. Dinah was interviewing the elderly owner and his wife when Duke rolled in. "Mr. Jenkins knows all of his milk cows by name," Dinah informed Duke. "He says none are missing. Again the thieves took small stuff."

"Except for my milking machine," the old man put in. "It was brand-new."

"Who'd want to steal it, or rakes and hoes?" his wife asked, seeming bewildered.

"I'll give you a report form to submit to your insurance company," Dinah told the couple. "Mrs. Jenkins, you said it was after two when you heard squealing tires going from your lane to the main highway?" Dinah jotted a note and turned to Duke. "Again the thieves are long gone. I came the minute Mr. Jenkins phoned, and didn't pass a soul. If you'll list what's missing," she said, handing Mrs. Jenkins a form, "Duke will send out information to the sources we know who deal in used farm implements."

"Are you sure you didn't see a vehicle, Mrs. Jenkins?" Duke asked. "I see you reported being up for a drink of water when you heard a vehicle leave your lane."

"I saw the flash of headlights across the trees, too. That's how I knew someone went from our gravel road to the highway. Come to think of it, as high as the beam hit, it would've been a pickup. I see cars leave here after dark, people who buy our fresh milk or butter," she explained. "Car lights illuminate the snowberry bushes I planted at our entrance. Another thing...the lights were off and they turned them on at the curve. Everything was pitch-dark before."

Duke retrieved an area map from his console. "So if you didn't pass anyone, Dinah, it means between here and town they left the highway."

Mrs. Jenkins fetched them coffee. "Most of these fire roads are dead ends," Dinah said. "Two lead to other ranches that have been robbed. This one goes to Mick Danner's fishing resort. I talked to him when the Weaver ranch was hit. Mick's cabins were all rented for the summer, but in two- and three-day increments. So I ruled out his guests."

"We should revisit everyone," Duke said. "Granted, the timing and frequency of the thefts seem to point to the perpetrators being locals. They'd guess when Mrs. Jenkins turned on a house light she'd call you, Dinah. They'd assume one of us would drive out from town. It'd be simple for them to pull down a fire road and wait for us to pass. Hopefully this time someone saw them."

"Okay, you take one side of the highway. I'll take the other. We'll convene back at the office. I hate to get people out of bed. On the other hand, ranchers and fishermen are probably up." She checked her watch.

THEY MET IN THE OFFICE a little over an hour later. "I can see by your face you didn't have any luck," Dinah said, flopping down in her chair. "Me, neither. It's as if these jokers are ghosts."

"Shall we run over to the Number 1 Diner for breakfast? I saw Sierra turn the Closed sign to Open as I parked," Duke said.

"Sure. You know her aunt Jordan is living with her? It must be hard for both of them. Her aunt is blind and Sierra doesn't seem her usual perky self."

"There's a lot of that going around. Beau and I said the same thing about Austin. He acted strange the whole Bozeman trip."

"How so?" Dinah acted interested.

"I expected him to help me drive, but no, he slept. He opted out of joining us for steak and beer. But he put in good rides."

"He broods, I've noticed," she said as they entered the restaurant already filling up with regulars. Dinah and Duke claimed stools at the counter. Both ordered coffee and cinnamon rolls.

"I don't need these calories," Dinah said when Irene Black set a giant, piping hot roll in front of her.

Duke said nothing, but picked up his fork and dived in.

"Did anyone you interviewed this morning complain about us not solving this case?" she asked Duke. "Remember my term as sheriff is up in January. Maybe I won't be reelected. Darn it, I think I'm good at this job."

Duke considered her words. Another sheriff might not keep him on. "Soon as the fair is over and visitors clear out from the rodeo, we need to start your campaign. Meanwhile we'll do everything possible to catch the thieves and locate Midnight."

"Yeah. You haven't forgotten my class? I leave the last day of rodeo."

"At least you'll be here to help me supervise the Wild Pony Race."

"How's it going with the boys you're teaching? Pam told me yesterday she's hosting all of them Thursday night at a sleepover."

"Really?" Duke straightened and smiled.

Dinah studied him momentarily. "Why does that excite you?"

He shrugged, not about to tell her it excited him because it meant Angie would be free one whole night. Instead he said, "Tommy is a know-it-all who hogs the spotlight. Bobby and Luke listen, and try their best. Really, if those kids end up friends, the hassle with Tommy will be worth my time."

"Hmm. I don't think the boys' friendship would be why Mom said I should encourage you to take a greater interest in Luke's mom."

"She what?" Duke fumbled his fork.

Dinah grinned slyly and kept eating.

"Honestly! Can't a guy be nice to a neighbor and her kid without some people making a federal case out of it?"

Dinah wadded her napkin and held up her hands. "I'm only relaying Mom's directive. But it's fun watching you squirm." Sliding off her stool, Dinah tossed some bills by her plate and called goodbye to Sierra, who stood at the end of the counter straightening menus.

"Oh, hey, Dinah." Sierra seemed startled to see

Dinah. When Dinah got near enough, Sierra set down the menus and hugged her.

Duke joined them, and Sierra acted more surprised to see him. "I supposed you'd be off to a rodeo. Your dad said you'll probably make the bull riding finals. Congrats. We see Joshua most days at lunch or dinner."

"Really? My dad?" Duke looked disbelieving.

Irene came up with a question that took Sierra away. Dinah led the way out, with Duke following her. "My dad is someone else who's acting weird," he said. "Yesterday he said he's thinking of retiring. Now it seems he's wasting money driving to town for lunch every day. That's not like him."

"Maybe it's something in Roundup's water," Dinah mused.

Duke ruminated on it while he sent out emails with new lists of the Jenkinses' missing goods. His workday ended at noon. He took Zorro home to feed him, and spent time sorting through graphics that might work for Angie's website. By two o'clock he'd worked up the nerve to call and ask her for a date. He punched in her number before he could back out. Her phone rang and rang, and as he was about to hang up, she answered, sounding out of breath.

"Have I caught you at a bad time?"

"Who is this?"

"Duke...Adams," he threw in for good measure, as if she'd be acquainted with more than one Duke.

"Oh, sorry. I didn't recognize your voice. I was out checking in a new horse. A way underweight mare whose sides are welts of spur gouges. The Humane Society worker who delivered her said a manager for a stock contractor tried to make her buck. She's too starved to buck. That's what I mean about rodeo business sucking."

"Ouch. I believe we've had this discussion."

"We did. I'm sure you didn't call to get another lecture. I guess Pam contacted you to ask if you'd drop Luke at her place after Thursday's lesson. She'll bring all three boys out to Thunder Ranch. She's invited Luke to spend the night with the twins. If he's scattered at the lesson it's because he's already bouncing off the walls in excitement."

"Angie, I called to ask if you'd go to dinner and maybe dancing with me Thursday night."

Time ticked past, then she said, "You and me...like on a date?"

"Is that so unimaginable?"

"I...uh...haven't dated anyone since before Lucas was born."

"So, what do you say we give it a whirl? We can go to the Prime Rib and Fish House out at the river and maybe eat on the porch overlooking the water. I hear they have dancing now every night. I'm no Fred Astaire, but I can two-step enough to get by."

"Thank you, but I worry about not being home if Luke decides he doesn't like sleepovers. I could fix you dinner here," she offered, although it wasn't a very robust invitation.

"My plan was to give you a break, Angie. If you don't have a cell phone, you can give Lucas my number."

"I have to get a cell. Oh, eating out does sound fun. I'll need to feed and water all the animals first. And... is it dressy? I don't have anything fancy to wear, and I don't want to embarrass you."

"Angie, stop! You'd never embarrass me. Jeans are

fine. Be comfortable. We're about to swing into the fair and rodeo days. Western wear is—what's the phrase I'm looking for? I saw it in this morning's paper. Got it—'Montana chic.'"

She laughed, and the silvery sound shot goose bumps up Duke's spine. "I'll come at seven," he said quickly. "If you need help with the animals, I'll pitch in."

"Seven? Okay. I'll make sure Lucas has your phone number."

Duke found himself staring at the wall with a crazy grin, still clutching his phone in a sweating hand. He was equally rusty at asking a woman out. Perhaps Angie would have felt better if he'd told her that.

THURSDAY WITH THE KIDS went better, although Tommy still couldn't get on the pony even when Luke and Bobby managed to slow him down. Duke tried to show Tommy how to get lift in a flying mount, by demonstrating in an adjacent corral with a full-size running horse.

Luke and Bobby wanted to try, but Tommy blustered and he was good at manipulation, so he talked them out of attempting it. At session's end, the dust-caked boys buckled into Duke's pickup.

"We are so gonna lose," Bobby moaned.

"Because you two squirts can't hang on to the stupid pony." As usual Tommy placed all the blame on his brother and Luke.

Duke opened his mouth to chide Tommy, but it was Luke who said fiercely, "We're getting better, aren't we, Duke?"

"You are, indeed." What pleased Duke was the fact

Luke got that statement out with nary a stutter. "We can probably work in two more sessions next week if you fellows want to. The rodeo and pony race aren't until the following week, but the fair starts this weekend, and I'll be logging extra hours at my deputy job."

"We need to practice so we can beat Jeb Woolsey's team," Tommy said. "They're telling everyone they're going to take home the trophy."

"I just want to go and have fun, Tommy," his brother mumbled.

"It's no fun if you don't win a trophy to show everybody," Tommy insisted. "Those dumb ribbons they give out for participating are for sissies."

Duke noticed the smaller boys slumped in their seats after that. But Zorro, bless his big heart, commiserated. He licked Luke's and Bobby's ears. Duke thought it was telling that his dog left Tommy alone.

Once Duke dropped the boys off at Pam's and they agreed on times for two more outings, he spent a few hours at the office. He had the place to himself. Dinah was out checking side roads she and Duke had identified as possible spots thieves may have pulled off, looking for fresh tire tracks or beer cans or maybe identifiable cigarette butts.

Duke skipped lunch to go inspect an area where bleachers were being erected for the rodeo. The same volunteers set up booths for the fair, but the fairgrounds were the county's jurisdiction and the rodeo arena fell within Roundup's city limits. He passed the time with several helpers sprucing up the grounds. All hailed him a champion as they congratulated him on his NFR standing.

"A winning ride is seventy percent the bull you draw, and thirty percent luck," he joked with two of the workers.

"You're too modest," one guy called. "According to your brother it's 100 percent about skill."

"Well, or 100 percent loving to ride," Duke said, grinning from ear to ear before he meandered through the chutes and holding pens. Ranking was like whipped cream on a chocolate sundae, but the ride itself and the cheers of the crowd were exhilarating.

His tour of the grounds ended, and he headed home to get ready for his night out. Thought of his date with Angie gave him the same ripple of excitement as bull riding. On stepping from the shower he wished he'd taken time for a haircut. Haircuts weren't something he invested in until his hair reached too far under his collar. Usually, if he looked slightly shaggy it didn't bother him. He wondered, worried really, about how Angie would view a slightly unkempt cowboy.

He knew she was one person not impressed by his bull-riding ranking. But, looking in the mirror, he admitted that he hoped to make a good impression on her.

Probably for the first time in history, he didn't study his closet full of black T-shirts and worn jeans and think his wardrobe was fine. Still, he had assured Angie it was okay to be casual. One concession he made to look special, he put on a belt with one of his winning buckles depicting a bull rider and fairly new handmade boots.

Zorro acted miffed to be left behind when Duke grabbed his wallet, keys and hat and ordered his pet to stay. Boy, howdy, but that showed how this evening was out of the ordinary. He rarely went anywhere without Zorro.

LATE IN THE AFTERNOON Angie fed and watered her menagerie. It felt odd not to have Luke chattering at her heels. From the day he was born, except when he went to school, he rarely was out of her sight. Admittedly she wasn't prepared for her son to become less dependent, and to spend more time at sports or things that took him away from her. Long ago she'd scratched marriage from her long-term life plan; after she'd been let down by Luke's jerk of a father. *The sperm donor.*

This date tonight with Dylan Adams was probably another error. She should have refused. But darn it, if you dangled a carrot in front of a horse long enough, you could tempt the animal to follow you anywhere. An evening of dinner and dancing had been Dylan's carrot, and she'd snapped up his bait.

He wasn't due to pick her up for another hour. She still had time to call him and cancel out, her voice of reason pestered.

She could make a lot of headway readying her new quarters to make large batches of horse treats. After all, she'd forked over forty hard-earned dollars to take a booth at the fair. It'd be her first time. In line to book her booth, she'd met Austin Wright's sister, Cheyenne, who planned to sell her handcrafted jewelry. Cheyenne's twin girls were so cute. In all the times Angie had been in and out of Austin's store she hadn't known until lately that he had a sister. Gramps said Austin's dad, Buddy, was once the town drunk. And he'd spent time in jail. Angie couldn't remember what for. But he must have reformed, because Cheyenne said she and the girls were living with him. The little girls were shy. But that day, Luke hid behind her, too. Since their booths ended up

across from each other, Angie hoped she and Cheyenne
might get to know each other better.

She missed having girlfriends. In Texas, as a waitress for a big, busy restaurant that catered to cowboys
and rodeo jockeys, she'd had girlfriends galore—
workmates. All of them had dropped her after she'd
left Carter Gray. That was how popular rodeo stars
were at the Lonesome Coyote restaurant.

So what on earth possessed her to get friendly with
another rodeo jock? Her voice of reason turned canny,
whispering inside her head—*Because Dylan Adams is
tall, lean and sinfully good-looking. Because he's soft-
spoken and caring. But the biggest reason of all—he's
so good with Luke.* It gave Dylan an A-plus-plus in
Angie's book.

In her bedroom she shed her work clothes and show-
ered. If this was going to be their one and only date—
and it was—what did it matter what she wore? *It just
does.* Pride made her want to look good; made her want
to see Dylan drool a little.

She owned one pair of black jeans with silver-studded
bling in a spray across back pockets that hugged her
derriere. She had a white tank top cut deeper around
the shoulders in back. Angie remembered the clerk saying when she bought the top in several colors that the
style looked sexy on her. Did she want to look sexy?
Heck, yes!

She rarely wore jewelry. The last time her grandfather had taken ill, he'd given her a narrow silver chain
with a small cross that had belonged to her grandmother. Angie wore it a few times to church, but always put it away afterward for fear she'd lose it. Pulling
it out now, she decided it went well with the plain shirt,

and drew together the silver on her jeans and silver toe-clips on her one pair of Sunday boots.

Oh, her hair. She stuck her tongue out at her mirror's reflection. Should she braid her hair or not?

Dylan decided that dilemma for her by pulling in ten minutes early. She left her hair loose and quickly slicked pink sheen across her lips then dashed for the door.

Yep, her decision on clothes was right on if the way Dylan snatched off his hat, did a noticeable double take and fanned his face as she stood in the doorway was any indication.

"Don't you look ready to paint the town red," he said, slowly taking in every inch of her.

"Not too red." She laughed, but gripped the door frame. "I meant it when I said I was out of practice at this dating stuff, Dylan."

"What kind of practice does it take to order off a menu and eat?" he asked in all seriousness.

"You're right. I'm ready to go if you are. Will I need a sweater?"

"Maybe, if we get seated on the porch. I probably should have called and reserved a table. So there you are, I'm out of practice, too."

She plucked a black cardigan from a row of pegs near the door, and tucked a few items in her jeans pockets. "You have your cell phone? I put your number on sticky notes in three places in Luke's backpack."

"I have it." And indeed it bulged in his pocket. "How's the little guy getting along at his sleepover?" Duke set a hand at the small of Angie's back and ush-ered her to his pickup where he took her elbow and as-sisted her into his tall vehicle. The fact the big Ford had oversized tires made it more difficult to climb into, especially for someone as petite as Angie.

Her hand and the flesh of her back beneath her thin tank top tingled from the lingering warmth of his fingers. "Luke didn't call me," she said, wrinkling her nose. "But I checked on him twice, which should tell you who's the more apprehensive about his first overnighter. Pam understood. First time I phoned the kids were playing Nintendo. The second time they were barbecuing hot dogs. Pam called Luke a delight. That's music to a mother's ears," Angie said, lifting her hair to one side while she bent to fasten her seat belt.

Duke sat staring at her, one hand on the wheel, the other on the ignition key.

Their gazes collided. "Is something wrong with your pickup?" she asked.

"No, nothing." He cranked the engine over with a roar. "I like your hair down. I thought I preferred it braided best, because it reminded me of winters when I was a kid. Ace and Colt braided bull ropes around a fire burning in Aunt Sarah's big fireplace. Each guy tried to outdo the other by coming up with fancier styles—like you don't always braid your hair the same way. Well, shoot," he muttered as he noticed Angie gazing bemusedly at him. "I meant that as a compliment. You probably don't think it's high praise to have your hair compared to a bull rope."

"I do. Coming from you it's refreshingly honest. I know how much you admire Ace, and your smile said it was a good memory." She relaxed into the brown leather seat. "You should smile more often, Dylan. Tell me more about your family traditions. In my family, we didn't stay anywhere long enough to carve out traditions."

Duke turned onto the highway that followed the river. Angie had rolled down her window, so he did the same and leaned an arm out. "The credit in our family all goes to Aunt Sarah. Her husband, John, and my dad, if it'd been up to them holidays would have been regular workdays. She doesn't decorate for every occasion the way she used to when us kids were little. Maybe she will again, you know, having grandkids. Holidays with all the trimmings are a big deal to kids."

Angie clamped her teeth over her lip. "I hope Luke doesn't feel cheated when he's your age and reminiscing." She rolled her head toward Duke. "Sadly too much of my time is taken up by work to decorate, or otherwise make a fuss over holidays except I cook a little more at Christmas."

"And that's exactly why we're having this night out," he said, swinging into a graveled parking lot that bordered a rustic log restaurant.

"I've never been out here. What a perfect setting with the evergreen trees and the river as a backdrop to the log restaurant."

"It's been here as long as I can remember. The high school held their proms here. I don't know if they still do."

"Did you attend your high school proms?" she asked him.

He shook his head. "Back then I was the same height I am now, but I had two left feet and was string-bean skinny. Did you go to yours? Girls always seem to make a big fuss over getting asked by the right boy and buying the right dress."

She didn't answer until they were almost at the door. "I was never popular, much to my mother's dismay. I didn't learn to dance until I was older. And it's been ages since I went to my last dinner-dance. I hope I don't step all over your feet."

The music was playing as they walked in. Duke felt Angie begin to sway, because he had his hand on her back. He asked for a table on the wraparound porch, and the hostess led them to a secluded spot. It also had easy access to double glass doors opening onto the dance floor.

"Do you want wine?" he asked her when the waiter handed him a wine list.

"Do you?" It was plain she was nervous again.

"I'm not into wine," Duke said. "I'll probably order a beer. If you prefer wine, I'll let you choose from the list."

"No, I'll have beer, too. With prime rib and a baked potato. Did you see how great that prime rib looked as we walked by?"

"Yes, and it's my choice, as well." The waiter returned and Duke ordered for them, except he let Angie pick her beer. They both asked for a dark lager, so the waiter delivered a pitcher.

"I fiddled around this afternoon with a couple of ideas for a possible logo for your website. I'll drop them by next week…. Which reminds me, Pam said her boys can practice Monday and Wednesday mornings."

"That'll work for me." They talked on, covering a variety of subjects. Superficial topics, nothing personal. Duke hoped she might warm up to the rodeo, but Angie always introduced something new instead of saying she planned to attend any of the riding events.

"This meal is scrumptious," she exclaimed halfway through. "It's truly a treat. I can't thank you enough. I almost called this afternoon and bailed on you. Nerves, I guess," she said with a shrug when Duke asked why.

The band heated up about the time they pushed their plates back. Duke split the beer left in the pitcher between them and invited her to dance.

He counted it in his favor that it was a slow, dreamy tune. He drew Angie close so their bodies fused. As the dance floor got more crowded, he tightened his hold.

When she leaned her cheek against his chest, Duke rested his chin on her soft hair. He savored how she fit against him. Not for the first time he imagined how sweet it would be to explore every inch of her smooth skin; how heavenly it would be to share their days and nights.

They'd both gotten into a languid groove of barely moving to tranquil tunes of the forties, when suddenly the beat shifted. "Everybody get set for line dancing," someone yelled. Because they were in the center of a packed floor, they were yanked into lines.

Laughing and clapping, they scooted and kicked to the ever increasingly faster pace played by the band.

Breaking once, Duke and Angie returned to their table where they polished off the warm beer. "I can't remember when I've had so much fun," Angie said, patting her hot face as Duke tucked his credit card into the bill folder. The waiter tried to talk them into dessert, but they both declined. So he took Duke's card and brought back copies for him to sign.

Angie collected her sweater and prepared to go. The band resumed, and the song was a slow rendition of Bon Jovi's "Make A Memory."

Duke held out his hand. "How about one last dance?"

Nodding, Angie smiled and stepped into his arms. Mellower now, Duke hummed along and nibbled the top of her ear. When the song ended, they wandered out to his pickup, arms twined around each other's waists.

All the way to her ranch, Angie felt the quiver of expectation knot her stomach.

Duke kept one hand on the steering wheel and thread his free hand with her fingers. They spoke little, but each basked in the glow left over from their last dance.

This part of a date Angie remembered. The thrum of her pulse, the longing she felt deep inside to take touching further. She remembered, too, the day she swore off men. But this was Dylan, and he didn't try flattery to talk her into bed.

In fact, he walked her to her door, and Angie knew he'd leave if she requested. Then he kissed her. His kiss didn't demand, but neither was it a friendly brush of lips like his first. Now his long, warm body pressed her against the door.

Angie's nerves jumped as she felt every surge to his lower body. Leaning into his kiss, she eased his T-shirt out from under his belt, and moaned at the sensation of his smooth skin beneath her palms.

One of his big hands covered her breast and she gloried in the friction of her tank top's soft fabric on her nipple.

The heat, the sizzle of the night, was suddenly broken by the blare of a raucous song spewing from between their bodies.

"My phone," Duke grated. Plainly he fought for control as he braced one muscled arm against the door casing and worked the phone out of his jeans with two fingers.

"'Lo," he growled even as he saw Angie stiffen, rake back her hair, and heard her loudly whisper, "Oh, my God, is it Luke? It is, isn't it?" She sounded panicky.

"Dinah," Duke spoke his caller's name for the benefit of the woman he'd been enjoying kissing on her doorstep. "Another break-in? No, no, you're not interrupting anything," he said, grimacing. "Where? The Walker ranch on Upper River Road? I'll meet you there." He clicked off and shot Angie an apologetic look.

Sagging against the siding, she lifted a hand and waved him away. "That call saved us from taking a very wrong turn. Good night, Dylan." She quickly opened her door with a shaking hand.

It wasn't until after she had disappeared inside and shut the door that Duke realized she'd gone off and left her house unlocked when there were all these damned break-ins in her area. She wouldn't like it, but he intended to take up that issue with her—after which he'd do his level best to convince her it had been a very *right* turn they'd nearly taken.

Chapter Nine

Upper River Road crossed a tributary of the Musselshell River and looped around downtown. Along it were various scenic pullouts. Duke drove past them in darkness, but he slowed and shone his pickup's side spotlight into secluded nooks he thought were large enough to conceal a vehicle. Other ranch roads bisected Upper River Road. A thief who knew them well could probably escape.

Duke reached the well-lit Walker ranch without passing any traffic. On a weeknight, unless something big like a high school football game or the fair and rodeo kept them out late, most ranchers were up at dawn.

Dinah and Loren Walker stood outside near his collection of barns and outbuildings. Walker bred and raised quarter horses. His was one of the larger ranches in the area. The pair watched Duke's approach as he left his Ford. Dinah ran a critical eye over him from his Sunday boots to the black Stetson she knew he saved for weddings and funerals. "Why are you all duded up?"

Ignoring her, Duke addressed Loren. "This is earlier than past thefts. What's missing? Any horses?"

"Don't think so. Sons o' guns scattered my mares," Loren said, stabbing a finger at the dark pasture that sloped into the foothills. "That's what brought me out of the house. Earlier I brought mares due to foal down from the high range to better keep an eye on them. I'd shut off the TV and was headed for bed when I heard hoofbeats and whinnying. I thought maybe a mountain cat was on the prowl, so I grabbed my rifle. I had to stop to step into boots or I bet'cha I'd have caught them in the act of ransacking my barn. They made off with saddles, bridles and several top-of-the-line ropes."

"You saw them or their vehicle, then?" Duke asked hopefully.

"Nope. I heard them peel out and hightail it to the highway. They used the windbreak from here to the main road as cover. They drove blacked out, no beams or taillights. I know from the sound it was a big engine."

Dinah hooked her thumbs in her back pockets. "That's not much help. Three-fourths of the county drive Silverados, Ford 450s or Jimmys, and their second cars are six-cylinder SUVs." She knelt and studied the ground. "I see a lot of tire tracks crisscrossing every which way. None look particularly new."

"This is getting annoying," Duke muttered. "I wish you'd shot out their tires, or even levered a few rounds over their heads. Maybe that would scare them into thinking twice about stealing around here. It ought to be getting harder for them to fence items with all the secondhand dealers on the lookout."

Walker unloaded his rifle and pocketed the shells. "Unless now they're stealing as a lark. If it's teens, they could stockpile their loot and keep stealing to show they can outsmart the law."

"That would burn my you-know-what," Dinah tossed out.

Loren shrugged. "Well, they're plenty bold. Dinah,

I'll let you know after daylight if any of my horses are gone. I don't think they were pulling a trailer. The last fifty feet of my access road is steep. With a trailer it wouldn't be a quick getaway."

Dinah closed her notebook. "That should make me feel better, but it doesn't. If Midnight's the only horse they took and he still hasn't surfaced, I worry about where—how they have him stashed."

Duke looked thoughtful. "You mean do they feed and exercise him the way a stallion needs? A horse with Midnight's energy isn't easily managed."

"It would serve them right if he stomped them to hell."

"Yeah. Are you going home or to the office?"

"Home. There's nothing more we can do from the office that can't wait until morning. What about you?" She had shaken hands with Loren, said she'd be in touch and walked with Duke to the vehicles. "As gussied up as you are, I still think I interrupted something big. And... you showed up here mighty quick. Another thing..." she paused for effect "...where is Zorro?"

Duke yanked open his pickup door. "Listen, Ms. Nosy, spend your supersleuthing skills on finding our thieves."

She laughed outright then smirked. "It didn't take much super sleuthing, as you put it, for me to add up facts. It's Thursday. Luke Barrington is spending the night at the Marshalls', which leaves Angie free all night. And you, dear cousin, besides being spiffed up, have never been able to lie worth a damn. But that's okay. Your secret is safe with me. I know how our family can tease a person to death. I keep telling my knot-head brothers it's why I'm still single, because they ribbed every guy I dated so bad, boyfriends decided I wasn't worth the effort."

"Is that true?" Duke shot her a sidelong glance. "I didn't do that, did I? If so, I apologize. So was there a particular boyfriend you wanted to keep?"

She sighed. "Not really. At least none I care to stand out here in the wilds discussing. By the way, I put a revised work schedule on your desk for the fair and rodeo. Let me know if you need any changes."

"Okay."

"We'll work regular hours tomorrow. Did you see the carnival crew haul in the midway rides today? They'll have the carnival operating by tomorrow night."

"I saw their rigs roll in. I supposed they wouldn't open until Saturday. I need Monday and Wednesday mornings off to work with the boys and the ponies."

"How's that going?"

"It'd be better if Tommy wasn't so full of himself."

"I did warn you. Hey, buzz me if you see anything suspicious driving home. Providing you're going home and not out to spend the rest of the night at the rescue ranch," she drawled, looking at Duke to see if she'd get a rise out of him.

"Good try, Dinah. I'm going home. But because I don't care who knows it, I did take Angie to the Prime Rib and Fish House for dinner and dancing tonight. I'd just driven her home when you called. Now, have I satisfied your curiosity?"

Dinah paused half in, half out of her vehicle. "I jabbed at you, but I admit I'm surprised. You've always been the family loner. Jeez, Duke, if you go and get married like Ace and Colt, I'll be the old, single member of the family."

"One date is far from marriage and you've left out Beau and Tuf. But if you're old, I'm purple. Hey, maybe you'll meet Mr. Right in Billings at a workshop...unless you intimidate all the guys in the advanced firearms class."

Dinah switched on her lights. "I can outshoot most guys at the shooting range. Frankly, if I have to dumb down at anything to interest a man, I am so going to remain single until I'm hobbling about with a cane."

Amused, Duke laughed as he cranked over his engine. He drove out ahead of her, but then he thought about what she'd said. No one in the family would want her to dumb down to attract a man. Ace bragged that she was gutsy. Like Colt and Beau, he maybe teased her, but they'd take on anyone outside the family who gave her grief. If Tuf were back, he'd champion his sister. That started Duke wondering again if his aunt or Ace had heard from the youngest Hart. Tuf got his nickname by being a scrapper. When it came to rodeo, he could ride anything. After he'd graduated they'd all bet he'd win the all-around. But he up and joined the Marines.

The family couldn't be prouder of him, but it didn't mean they weren't also all worried about why he wasn't coming home.

Preferring to not end his fantastic night with Angie on such a somber note, Duke shifted back to imagining how his night may have ended had Dinah not phoned when she did. That more pleasant image lingered until he got home to be greeted by Zorro's sloppy doggie kisses. They certainly didn't compete with kissing Angie.

To work off excess energy his memories stoked, Duke took Zorro out for a run.

THE NEXT TWO DAYS DUKE SPENT his free mornings pulling together ideas to promote Angie's horse-cookie business on the web. He couldn't wait to give her some possibilities to look at. He was partial to graphics depicting a horse. His favorite was more a cartoon where the horse was plainly chewing something and smiling. Another, more traditional image showed a silhouette of a disembodied hand feeding a horse. He ended up printing both, and working them in with her AB logo.

Before he left for his job Saturday, he phoned Angie. She didn't answer at the house, so he loaded the laptop he planned to give her and swung past her ranch, assuming she'd be out on the property. Her vehicle was gone and her house quiet.

He thought she could be at her new shop, but he didn't really have time to go there, so he wrote her a note saying to call him if she had questions, and left the bag of items by her kitchen door.

Off and on while he patrolled, he made a point of trying her home number to no avail. Late in the day he gave up, figuring he'd offer to drive his aunt to church the next morning where he'd surely catch Angie.

"MOM, THIS DUMB OLD FAIR is bo-r-ring. Do we gotta do this every day? Why do I hafta stay in the b-booth?" Luke whined, but stuttered minimally.

"Honey, I can't let you wander around the fairgrounds alone. There are more people here than I ever imagined would come to Roundup. I know you're dying to go on the rides. How about if I ask Bobby and Tommy's mom if she plans to take the boys? Maybe she'd let you go along."

Luke flopped back down on one of the folding chairs

Angie had brought for each of them to sit on during slow times. A flurry of customers came up to buy horse cookies, or learn about them. The minute they all left, Luke popped up again. "You can call Duke on your new cell phone. M-maybe he'd take me on rides."

"Luke, we can't bother him when he's working." She felt her cheeks flame a bit, recalling how they'd parted Thursday night. "Uh, since you mentioned my new phone, I need to write down the number for you to carry with you." Angie tore off a piece of paper and scrawled the number. "Don't lose this, Lucas. Now you can reach me anytime."

Luke took the paper and stuffed it in his pocket. "How many days are we gonna be here?" he asked again.

"The fair runs from now through the end of the rodeo."

"B-but we get t-to see the rodeo, right?"

Angie turned aside and sold two packets of horse treats to a local rancher. "Luke, you know I am not a fan of rodeos," she said after the customer left. "I thought maybe you could go to the pony race with Pam."

"Aw!" Luke slumped in his seat. "I want you to watch me. And Duke's gonna ride a bull. So is his b-brother. His cousin Colt rides buckin' horses l-like my d-dad. Bobby said everybody goes, 'cause the rodeo is cool, Mom."

"Lucas," Angie said, "many rodeo animals are ill-treated. There are plenty of careers more worth thinking are cool." She decided it was probably best to not make an issue out of his mentioning his father.

Luke's lip stuck out stubbornly.

As Angie was thinking about phoning Pam Marshall, she walked up without her twins. "Hi, Angie. I came to ask if Monday morning I can pick Luke up here before driving the kids to Thunder Ranch? I'm paying my neighbor to sell my birdhouses in my booth, to give me a break."

"That's fine with me. Thanks for chauffeuring. By the way, I told Luke I'd ask if you plan to take your boys to the midway. Luke is dying to go, but this being my first time selling at the fair, I need all the hours here I can get."

"Would Monday evening work for you? Gary took the boys to Ryegate to visit his mother who is just home from the hospital today. Tomorrow is church."

"Any time it's convenient for you. I've been busier than I thought. I'm not complaining. Only I assumed I'd have a bit more free time."

"Our fair and rodeo are gaining popularity. I read they expect double the crowd over last year. Well, I have to run. Truthfully, I spotted a copper necklace across the way at Cheyenne Sundell's booth, but I waffled over buying it. Now I want it, and I'm afraid if I don't hurry back it'll be gone."

They parted and Angie resumed a brisk business all afternoon. Tired as she felt at the close of the day, she knew she had to bake for half the night to keep ahead of sales. Not that it was a bad thing. Selling out every day would be terrific.

On arriving home she found the bag Dylan had left at her door. While supper cooked, she called to thank him. His cell was busy, so she left a message. "Dylan, it's kind of you to bring me all of this material, but I'm swamped at the moment and won't have a chance to delve into it for a few days. How about if I give you a call when I do? I'm going to the shop tonight to bake. The ovens there are bigger and I have more room to spread cookies out to cool."

DUKE WAS SORRY HE MISSED Angie's call. By the time he had a minute to phone her back, there was no answer. He decided to skip his supper break and run by her shop.

Pulling in next to her vehicle, he could see her inside. He found the front door locked, which was good. He rapped on the glass, and Lucas came running.

"Duke, hi. How did'ya know we were here? Can Zorro come in and play?"

"Uh, it's up to your mother."

Angie came to the door of the kitchen. "Hi, Dylan. What are you doing here?" She had an oven mitt on one hand and a large spatula in the other.

"I got your message and came by to see if I could help mix or bake or something for an hour."

"Really?" She was plainly surprised.

"Oh, man!" Luke complained, kicking at a chair leg that sat in the space where Ruby used to serve coffee and doughnuts.

Duke glanced at the boy and remembered what it was like having his dad busy all the time. "I see you were reading."

Angie saw Zorro stick his nose in the door. "Luke, if you two sit right where you are on the floor you can read the new book we bought you to Zorro."

"He'll like it," the boy said, running to get the book. "It's about a dog that rides ferry boats in— Where is that state, Mom?"

"Washington State," she said.

Boy and dog plopped down next to each other, and Duke smiled.

"I have to hire helpers to work here, but I haven't had time to interview," Angie said.

Duke rolled up his sleeves. "What can I do?"

"If you're serious, you can grate apples and carrots."

"I am. You have flour on your nose," he said, brushing it off, then bending to kiss where he'd brushed.

"Dylan." Angie ducked away. "We can't get involved," she said in hushed tones.

"Why not?" He stepped around her, washed his hands at the sink, then picked up the large grater and dipped into the bowl of peeled apples.

"You know why. I'm just having a hard time getting used to the fact you and your whole family are profiting from rodeo."

He felt a zap of disappointment. Rodeo was a huge part of his life. He wanted her to like it. "I'll get you and Luke tickets to sit with Aunt Sarah and my family. Maybe you'll change your mind."

"Doubtful. Don't waste your money. I'm not planning to go at all."

He grabbed two carrots and grated them into a large bowl. "You can't mean you'll skip watching Luke. He'd be really hurt," he said softly so the boy in the next room wouldn't hear.

She glanced up from bagging cookies and stared at him. "I should have never signed him up in the first place. All right. I'll arrange to attend his event. But if one pony gets mistreated, that's the end of it."

It wasn't much, but it was something. Duke worked his hour feeling as if there was wiggle room to change her mind.

"Time to head back on patrol at the midway," he said, passing her a full bowl.

She tried to take it out of his hands, but he tugged on it until she was near enough so he could kiss her again. He took his time, and felt his heart start to speed when she didn't pull back instantly, and in fact she kissed him back.

When she finally broke the connection, Duke stepped to the door. "Don't stay here too late. I'll try to get those tickets tomorrow." He stopped to ruffle Luke's hair.

"You're doing much better at reading, kid."

The boy grinned happily and gave Zorro a last hug.

Duke whistled on his way out, satisfied he'd left Angie speechless for once.

The midway kept him hopping until midnight, and the bars did a brisk business with liquor flowing until 2:00 a.m.

Dead on his feet at the end of his lengthy shift, he listened again to Angie's message on his cell phone, just to hear her voice before he slept.

The next day was Sunday. He'd see her at church.

That was his hope until he played a message from Dinah he'd missed that came in on his answering machine. "Duke, I need you to cover my shift Sunday morning. I got a call from a secondhand farm implement dealer in Grass Range. He may have the Jenkinses' stolen milking machine, of all things. I collected a brochure on the machine from Mr. Jenkins, and I'm meeting the shop owner at nine. This could be the break we need."

"Dang, Zorro. I'll have to take Angie the rodeo tickets later." He knew he should cross his fingers that

Dinah had luck in Grass Range. But he didn't want Angie to have time to think about refusing the tickets.

His Sunday passed in a flurry of activity. Several times that morning Duke headed out to check out the fairgrounds. Minor incidents at the midway kept diverting him. Thankfully none were too serious.

Dinah made it back later than she hoped, so Duke pulled double duty.

"Hey," he said, meeting her coming into the office as he was about to go to the diner for supper. "Tell me it was our missing milking machine and you can close this case."

She tossed her keys on top of her desk and unclipped the belt that held her handgun, nightstick and handcuffs. Flinging herself into her chair, she blew out a disgusted breath. "It was the right machine, but our burglars pulled a fast one. They hired a kid to go in and sell it and other items from the Jenkins farm. I tracked down the kid, a local teen. Our thieves paid him twenty-five bucks to do their dirty work."

"Did he describe the guys who hired him?"

"The boy is mentally challenged. The store owner said he came in with the items and a note indicating a relative needed cash to pay a doctor bill. After the transaction, the owner's wife, who'd seen your last flyer, had her husband call the boy's family. There were no relatives in dire straits."

Duke lifted his hat and rubbed the back of his neck. "What kind of creeps steal from nice old folks, then compound their dirty deed by using a handicapped kid?"

"Somebody I hope we find and prosecute," Dinah said. "And if they've hurt Midnight, I'll personally make it my mission to see the book is thrown at them. My new concern is that we're dealing with people without a conscience."

"That makes it more urgent to run them down and find Midnight. Aunt Sarah is afraid he's gone for good. I still have faith he'll turn up."

"I wish Ace had insured him," Dinah said. "Flynn told me it was too costly. Ace elected to wait until Midnight produced a string of foals."

"Hindsight's always twenty-twenty. But it's the horse they want back, not the money. Hey, I left you names of drunks I issued warnings to. Catch them again and you can throw their hineys in jail overnight. That's what I told them."

"I don't recognize any of these names. Are cowboys showing up early for the rodeo?"

"Yep, and now the midway and both saloons are all yours, boss. I was going to go eat, but I think I'll head home and hit the sack. In the morning I'm with the wild-pony racers again."

"Does Angie appreciate all you're doing?"

He paused with a hand on the door. "No. She doesn't like rodeos and wishes she hadn't let Luke participate."

"Wow. Is that why she's never been overly social? Now, don't hop all over me for saying that. Ask our friends. Most of our crowd would ask, Angie who?"

"Give her a break. She came to a new town, pregnant and unmarried. She had a kid to raise, a ranch to run and her grandpa got sick. Did anyone we know offer to help her out?"

"I can see this gets you all worked up, Duke. Go on home. Our job will only get hotter the more cowboys roll in. Oh, one more question…. Is Angie afraid Luke's daddy will show up at our rodeo?"

"Dammit, Dinah, you know more about her than you let on."

"Just asking—if he pops in will she welcome him back? I'm worried about you getting in too deep and maybe getting your heart broken."

"No." Duke started to say more, but in deference to not gossiping about Angie, he yanked open the door and stalked out. "Just…no!" he reiterated before slamming it hard.

He went home and thought long and hard about calling Angie before he went to bed. In the end, he didn't want to risk a conversation on a topic bound to upset her. He had to believe she'd meant it when she'd said Luke's father was out of her life for good.

PAM BROUGHT THE THREE BOYS to Thunder Ranch for their lesson. "I'll be back in two hours to collect them," she called before Duke had a chance to ask where Angie was this morning.

The boys performed a bit better and were superexcited. "We're going to the fair tonight," Bobby announced as they ended the session.

"All of you?" Duke's gaze strayed to Luke.

"Yes, our mom is taking us. I can't wait to ride on the Ferris wheel," Bobby exclaimed.

"Your mom isn't going?" Duke pressed Luke.

"She's t-too busy."

"I know," Duke said. "I wondered if she'd set up her online business using the stuff I left her."

Luke shrugged and darted off as Pam pulled in and honked. But he turned back and dug in his pocket.

"Mom got a cell phone," he said, only stuttering as he added, "H-here's the n-number." He left the paper with Duke and raced back to the SUV before Duke could jot it down and return the paper.

Besides, Tommy Marshall yelled for Luke to hurry.

Duke stared at the number even as dust from Pam's departure blew over him. He wondered why Angie hadn't felt the need to inform him she'd gotten a cell phone?

He didn't have long to waste worrying. His day as deputy began with Dinah leaving him a note saying he needed to check all of the permits posted for the midway rides. Apparently a city council member said the number of permits issued didn't match the number of rides the fair crew had set up.

It was late by the time Duke figured out the councilman was wrong. He called for a to-go meal from the Number 1 Diner and ran past to pick it up. As he paid at the register, he noticed his dad seated at a back table with the woman Duke remembered seeing as she got off a bus a few weeks ago. Her name was Jordan and she was Sierra Byrne's aunt. Duke would have gone over to say hello, but something in the way the couple laughed together, their heads nearly touching, gave him pause. That and he'd left Zorro in the office.

Back at the office, he fed Zorro and ate his meal while sorting through new warrants. Some were for deadbeat cowboy dads who might turn up to ride in the rodeo. Duke wondered how a man could bail out on support payments for his children. He had to hand it to Colt for meeting his obligations when it wasn't always easy.

Suddenly he looked up and realized Zorro was whining. Duke rolled back in his chair about the time Zorro barked several times and leaped at the window, rattling the vertical miniblinds.

"What is it, boy?" Duke pulled aside the blind as the dog yipped and thumped his tail excitedly. It was dusk and it took time for Duke's eyes to adjust. Once they did, he was surprised to see Luke Barrington trudging down the sidewalk. He wore dark jeans, a navy sweatshirt and carried a backpack. Luke stopped on the sidewalk next to the sign for the bus stop, and seemed to be squinting up at it.

Duke's heart ticked up in anticipation of seeing Angie as he leaned into the glass. Across the street customers entered the diner, but this side of the street was empty except for Luke.

Because Zorro bounced against the door, Duke opened it. His pet shot out, but Duke followed more slowly. By the time he reached Luke, the boy had flung his arms around Zorro. In the faint light shed by a streetlamp, Duke saw streaks of old tears on Luke's freckled cheeks.

"Hey, little guy, where are you headed?"

"T-Texas," the boy stuttered.

"Uh, Texas is a far piece from here. Let's sit a minute and talk this over." Duke gestured to a bench under the sign.

Luke's fingers curled into Zorro's thick fur. "'Kay," he said, but tugged the dog along to where he could perch on the very edge of the bench and still keep one hand on the shepherd. Stuttering more, Luke finally got out that he was running away.

Duke didn't sit, but propped one boot on the bench. "Your mom's gonna be sad, Lucas. Is she in town? Maybe at the feed store or the Western-wear shop?"

"At the fair. She's prob'ly at her booth s-selling horse treats."

"Does she know you're off to Texas?"

Luke shook his head. "I'm spo'sed to be with Bobby and T-Tommy and their mom," he stammered. "Mrs. Marshall took us to the rides. Tommy called me a baby 'cause I didn't want to ride on the Twister. Then he said my dad never ever wanted me 'cause I'm such a loser. And that's why my mom moved to M-Montana. Tommy said everybody at school kn-knows. So, I'm gonna find my dad and prove Tommy's lying."

It took the boy so long to get that entire block of information out, Duke began to get more worried. By now Pam would be frantic, and Angie, as well.

"Since Texas is a long trek, what do you say I buy you a hamburger and milkshake to tide you over? The diner's right across the street."

"I am h-hungry. Bobby said we couldn't eat b'fore the rides, or else we'd puke."

Duke rubbed a thumb down the center of his forehead, and thought, *Bless Bobby.* "Tell you what, pardner, let me grab my wallet and lock the sheriff's office. You sit right here and hang on to Zorro."

Luke bobbed his head and tightened his grip on the dog who acted happy to have a human attached.

Rushing into the office, Duke fumbled in his wallet for Angie's cell number that thankfully Lucas had given him that morning. He punched it in and impatiently waited for a connection. "Angie, it's Duke."

"Sorry, I can't talk. I'm at the fairgrounds searching for Lucas. Pam took the boys on rides, and something happened. Luke should have come back to my booth, but he didn't." She sounded close to tears and Duke's heart wrenched.

"He's here, Angie. In town. He's sitting outside my office with Zorro. We can talk later about why he took off, but the upshot is I promised to take him to the Number 1 Diner for a burger and shake. Can you come there?"

"In town? He walked all that way? Oh, my God. Why would he do that? He's normally a responsible kid. Never mind. Of course I'll come right away."

"Tommy told Luke his dad didn't want him," Duke said. "Luke decided to go to Texas to find his father and learn the truth. Maybe it's time you level with him about his dad. I don't want to interfere, Angie, but he's hurting."

Duke wasn't sure she hadn't hung up, when she said, "It's nothing I wanted to talk to him about until he was older. I suppose that was wrong." She sighed. "I'll be there as soon as I find Pam and let her know Luke's okay. Goodness, Tommy is already in trouble. I don't think Pam will let him be in the pony race, and Luke will be disappointed about that, too. Or maybe not if he was running away. What a mess, Dylan. But thank you."

"Don't mention it. See you soon." He tucked his phone and her number in his pocket again and left to collect Luke.

Crossing the street, Duke stopped outside the diner to snap Zorro's leash to an old hitching post. He ushered the boy inside and chose a table near the back of the restaurant. He sat Luke facing the door where he'd see Angie when she came in. The kid deserved a chance to figure what he'd tell his mother.

Duke noticed as they waited for burgers that Luke's

eyes kept drifting shut. "Are you tuckered out?" he asked. "It's quite a hike to town from the fairgrounds."

"Yeah, and I have heavy b-books in my b-backpack." Luke slurped his chocolate shake.

"It was dangerous to walk to town, Luke. There are no sidewalks and drivers can't see well as the sun sets. You can't let Tommy's taunts, or anyone else's, make you do something unsafe. You know that part will worry your mom."

"Probably. But…she didn't hear T-Tommy. He…he made fun of how I t-talk."

"Luke, listen. When I was your age I stuttered just like you. My cousin Ace helped me speak slower and to think beforehand. Your mom said when school starts you'll take speech therapy. That will turn things around for you."

Luke's eyes had widened when Duke confessed his old problem. "You talk good now. Wow, maybe I'll get better."

"You will."

"Uh-oh." Luke slid down in his chair, and Duke turned and saw Angie rush into the diner. She charged straight up to their table and hugged her son until Duke pulled out a chair for her, and she sat, but continued clinging to Luke. "You scared me half to death, Luke. I thought we were a team, you and me."

"I'm sorry. T-Tommy…" the boy tried, but his eyes filled with big fat tears that splashed on the table.

Chapter Ten

Angie's chin trembled. She released Luke's arm and ran her fingers through his hair. "Oh, Lucas, I know what Tommy did. He was wrong to pick on you, but it's partly my fault. I should have anticipated when you started school that you'd get questions about your father. We had Gramps, so I hoped it wouldn't be an issue. But I guess kids hear stuff adults say when they aren't aware their kids are listening."

"Huh?" Luke's expression was one of greater confusion. Then their meals were delivered, and he ducked away from his mother and bit into his burger.

The waitress asked if Angie wanted to order. Still dazed from the fright of her life, she gazed blankly at the girl.

Duke nudged her foot. "I doubt you ate anything at the fair. If you don't want a burger, try soup and a sandwich. It's tomato soup, and turkey salad on one of Sierra's fresh-baked rolls."

"That sounds good," Angie said weakly. The minute the waitress took off, Angie pulled her chair closer to the table. After two false starts she began her story anew. "Luke, honey, before I even knew I was going to have you, I split up with the man who is your father. It may be hard for you to understand, but he and I began a relationship with huge differences between us."

"Like what?" Luke asked as he squeezed ketchup on his fries.

Angie cast a surreptitious glance at the man feigning interest in his hamburger, then knotted her hands. "Ah... Carter was a rodeo champion when we met. But he and others used spurs on horses they rode. I objected, and he promised if I moved in with him he'd quit the rodeo and we'd get married. He said he'd been offered a job on a ranch near Fort Worth. Maybe two weeks after I moved in I found out there was no job, and he'd entered a slew of new rodeos. I packed my things and left, and got my old job back. Then I learned I was pregnant. I felt I had to tell him. People who knew us both thought I told him so he'd take me back. The truth is I wouldn't have gone back because of his lies. Plus, by then he'd told mutual friends he didn't want me and never had any intention of us getting married."

Her soup and sandwich came, and she dipped the spoon into her soup, but let it rest there.

Duke's mind flashed through rodeo stats and he guessed she had hooked up with Carter Gray. From all he had heard on the circuit about the bronc rider, Duke had no trouble believing all Angie said.

"But if you told him about me then T-Tommy was r-right, my dad didn't w-want me," Luke said, his face crumpling.

Duke slid a big hand around the boy's narrow shoulders. "Luke, not all cowboys are cut out to be dads."

The boy looked up with teary eyes, and to Duke's shock he asked without stuttering once, "Duke, are you cut out to be one? A dad?"

Duke looked Luke straight in the eye. "I sure like to think I have what it takes to love and care for a family," he said earnestly. "You've never met my twin brother, Beau. He and I grew up without a mom. Our dad worked long hours to support us. He pretty much had to be both mom and dad, like your mom is, Luke. I think I turned out okay."

Luke seemed to consider that as he polished off the last of his burger, all while studying Duke's face.

"Yup, Duke. You're real okay."

Angie bent over her meal until Luke wiped his mouth and addressed her. "Mom, he takes good care of Zorro, so don't you think Duke would be good with a family?"

She pushed aside her bowl. "I...ah...am sure Dylan would make an admirable family man, if not for..." she stopped, blinked, then muttered "...his obsession with riding bulls."

"I'm not obsessed," Duke defended. "It's a sport like any other."

"No. Your standing is big talk around the fair. Animals are not born to buck, I don't care what you say."

Across the table, Luke nodded off before Angie finished her damning statement.

"Don't wake him," Duke said, pulling out his wallet to drop money on the table. "He's out for the count. Would you like me to carry him to your vehicle?"

"Please," she said, changing gears. "He's a deadweight when he's asleep. I'm parked in this block." She picked up Luke's backpack.

Lifting the gangly boy, Duke racked his brain for something to say to counter Angie's words that were surely meant to drive him off. But he didn't want to pro-

voke an argument tonight. Later he would argue again
that bucking bulls weren't mistreated.

Angie's vehicle had a narrow backseat. Duke settled
Lucas and buckled him in, and when the boy sighed and
his head bobbled, Duke smiled and ruffled his blond
hair.

She stood by and shut the door. In spite of all the
negative comments she'd aimed at this cowboy in the
restaurant, he continued to do things that moved her.
Moved her enough for her to rise up on tiptoes and deliver a kiss that landed at the corner of his mouth.

"There are no words to convey how grateful I am for
all you did tonight, Dylan. I can't recall ever being as
scared as when Pam came to my booth looking for Luke
who should've been with her. I told myself Roundup is
a safe town. But…"

"It's okay, Angie. He's your whole world."

She kissed him again and got into her SUV and drove
off, leaving Duke standing at the curb with a hand to
his cheek where her last kiss still felt sweet.

Someone stepped up behind him and slapped Duke
on his back. "Well, well, well, old son, how long have
you been in a romantic relationship with Angie Barrington? And how is it I missed knowing?"

Whirling, wearing a scowl, Duke let out a sigh when
he identified his favorite cousin. "Ace, dang, you caught
me off guard." Duke opened his mouth to deny having
a romance with Angie, but because there was no one
he trusted more than Ace, he backed down. "I've admired her for quite a while, but we got closer because
I'm helping her son and the Marshall twins train for
the Wild Pony Race. Last week I finally asked Angie
out, but another burglary broke up our evening. The

kicker is, Ace, she harbors bad feelings for rodeos and rodeo cowboys."

"Huh, could've fooled me." Ace jerked a thumb toward a storefront whose proprietor lived above her shop. "I just finished a courtesy call to help whelp Miss Grogan's teacup poodle. I came down her back stairs and happened to see Angie kiss you twice, good buddy." Ace wiggled two fingers under Duke's nose.

"Kisses of gratitude," Duke said, sounding gloomy. "Tommy Marshall bedeviled Luke tonight about his lack of a dad. Luke ran away, but thanks to Zorro being alert, I intercepted him. That's all it was, Ace. Angie split up with her ex over him promising to quit rodeo, but he didn't follow through. I'm this close to reaching the finals." He held his thumb and forefinger barely apart. "Dang, I worked hard to get there. But…I want to convince Angie it's not the most important thing in my life. I know you squared differences with Flynn, so how about giving me some advice?"

Ace looked serious. "The only advice I can give is that any solution has to come from the heart. I'm confident you'll figure it out, Big D. Meanwhile, I left my ladylove at home preparing an intimate, romantic dinner for two." Grinning like a fool, Ace shifted his vet bag to the other hand and strode to where he'd parked his pickup.

Duke felt cut adrift and left in a quandary. He always could count before on Ace's guidance. Now his cousin's life had changed. His life, too. It was probably high time he stopped leaning on Ace.

Hands in pockets, he sauntered back to the diner, collected Zorro and drove out to make a last nightly check of the fair. Looking around at revelers out for a good time, it looked as if he was one of the few locals his age not paired up.

Then he ran into Austin Wright shooting corks at tin ducks running across the back of a carny's booth. "Hey there, it appears the ducks are winning," Duke said, laughing at the exasperated look on his friend's face.

"It's rigged. I thought I'd win my sister's kids a couple of those big pandas. I've already spent twenty bucks. I could probably buy the damned things cheaper."

Duke plopped down a twenty and picked up one of the cork guns. "You could, but it wouldn't be half as much fun, or as good on the old macho ego."

"Watch who you're calling old, Adams."

The men spent another twenty apiece, but they did walk away with a panda each. In the parking lot, Duke passed his bear to Austin. "Give this to Cheyenne with my good wishes."

"Hey, thanks. I suppose you'd give yours to Colt's kids."

"Well, he has two also, and if not for you I'd never have won one."

"Follow me to the shop and I'll brew a pot of coffee."

Duke glanced at his watch. It was midnight and he was off duty. The fair was closing for the night. "If I didn't have Zorro I'd say let's take these bad-dude bears and close down the Open Range Saloon with a couple of beers."

Austin stopped beside his battered pickup, and he seemed to weigh Duke's suggestion before he opened the lock and tossed the bears inside. "You probably shouldn't drink with your uniform on, Duke."

"You've got a point. And like I said, I have Zorro. Maybe I'll take a rain check on coffee. With the fair and rodeo on top of more ranch robberies, Dinah and

I have both been pulling long hours. And she's off to a conference in Billings next weekend, so I'll be the Lone Ranger, so to speak."

"Dinah's leaving town when half her family's competing at the rodeo? That's not very sporting of her."

"She'll only miss the last day." Duke hesitated, then decided to come right out with it. "Out of curiosity, what are you and Dinah feuding over?"

"I don't know what you mean."

"The other night when you were both in the office, I could have stuck a fork in the tension it was so thick."

"It's private, Duke. Reaches back to when Dinah and I vied for which of us was Roundup's most wild child, or wild teen."

"In that case I probably don't want to know. I hate keeping secrets. But I noticed you've registered to ride. If I don't see you again before rodeo starts, good luck."

"Same goes for you. It's always good to knock 'em dead in the hometown venue."

The men went their separate ways. Duke grinned watching Austin drive off with a pair of pandas looking big and bad and sharing his seat.

At home he had a call on his answering machine from Pam Marshall. She asked if she and her husband could meet with him the next day. Duke wouldn't blame them if they yanked Tommy from next week's competition. On the other hand, if they did it'd be a crushing blow to Bobby and Luke who'd worked hard and were about as excited at the prospect of the race as any kids Duke had ever seen.

IN THE MORNING ANGIE WAS exceptionally quiet. Sarah Hart, who'd come to feed and groom some of the small animals, took notice and said as much to Angie.

Because she was letting Luke sleep late, Angie dumped her yesterday's woes on a woman she counted as a good friend.

"My, you had quite a scare. Bless my nephew for being in the right place at the right time. You know, Angie, it's nothing I usually discuss, but my husband let down our boys when they were much older than Luke. Ace, Tuf and even Colt had difficulty dealing with finding out their dad wasn't the man they looked up to. At their ages they'll deal, but I know it affected each one adversely. I remain thankful John's problems didn't come to light while they were as young as Luke. Boys, especially, need that special bond with fathers."

Angie chewed her lip. "Dylan grew up without his mother. He told Luke last night that he and his twin turned out all right."

Sarah smiled. "I like to think I filled a needed gap. But Duke wasn't without problems. I'm just saying kids, boys, benefit when they have a man to bond with. Angie, I hate to rush through feeding the pets, but I'm scheduled to sell rodeo tickets in an hour. Have you gotten yours and Luke's tickets yet? You two need to sit with us."

"I haven't bought tickets." Angie didn't elaborate. She scattered the last of her corn out for the chickens and walked back to the house with Sarah, who then left.

Angie waved goodbye, but her mind worked overtime nibbling on Sarah's counsel. She'd seen how fast Luke bonded with Dylan. And truth be told, in spite of his involvement with rodeo, she was falling for him, too.

IN THE MORNING, AT THE FIRST decent hour Duke had free, he phoned the Marshall house. "Pam, it's Duke Adams.

Sorry I didn't get back to you last night, but I was on patrol until midnight. I don't go in today until noon, so I can come out now if you'd like."

"Good. I really wanted Gary in on this and he has a sales meeting he needs to attend this afternoon. We've just finished breakfast. Come now and join us for coffee. I'll send the boys out to pick the last of our corn. That will leave us free to talk."

The Marshalls lived about as far out on the opposite side of Roundup as Thunder Ranch was on the other. It took him twenty minutes to get there. The boys came out of the house, each carrying two bushel baskets. "Hi, Duke," Bobby said. "Dad said to send you into the kitchen." Bobby set down his basket and pointed to a door. "Can Zorro go to the cornfield with us?" he asked as he moved to pet the dog.

"Sure. But bring him back and put him in my pickup if he starts to chase crows. He can't catch them and crows can gang up on him."

Both boys promised to be careful.

Duke realized Tommy, the braggart, had been subdued when ordinarily he would have overshadowed his brother.

Duke removed his hat at the door. Gary rose and shook hands.

"What do you take in your coffee?" Pam asked him, getting up to fill another cup.

"Just black, thanks. I learned to drink it that way at the office where we were always running out of creamer." He sat in the empty chair. "I'm assuming we're going to talk about Tommy's transgressions from last night at the fair." Duke blew on his hot coffee.

Gary stirred sugar in his cup. "Pam's inclination is

to take him out of the pony race. She more or less told Angie that last night, and Angie said it's up to us. But you've been working with the boys, so we'd like your opinion."

"My first thought was to ground Tommy until he's twenty-one," Pam said wryly. "Pulling him from the race was my second choice."

Duke leaned back in his chair. "The thing is, that would punish Bobby and Luke, too, and they didn't do anything wrong."

"Exactly what I said." Gary laced both hands around his cup. "I'm disappointed in Tommy, and let him know it. I had a long talk with him about what he did wrong."

"One point in his favor," Pam said, "after that he volunteered to call Luke and apologize. I want to believe he is sincere. He's been a bit of a trial, and I don't want this very bad thing he did to pass without ramifications for him."

"I agree he needs a lesson," Gary put in.

"I have an idea to run by you," Duke said. "I told them at the beginning it's a race that relies on teamwork. Tommy convinced the other two boys he'd only participate if he could be the one to chase and try to mount the pony. But the truth is Luke and Bobby aren't heavy enough to dig in and hold the pony in check to allow Tommy time to climb aboard." Duke spread his hands, leaving his thoughts on the table.

It dawned on Gary first. "If Tommy has to give up the spot he wants to Luke, it will impress on him things won't go his way if he does wrong."

"I see value in that," Pam agreed. "I'll go along if Angie agrees. You've scheduled their last session at Thunder Ranch tomorrow. We'll have a heart-to-heart with him. If he honestly sees the error of his ways, we'll be out at ten. If he decides to be stubborn, he will have to explain to Luke and Bobby that he's the sole reason they have to withdraw from the race."

Confident Tommy was a good kid beneath all his bluster, Duke got up to leave as the boys came in with a farm wagon carrying their four bushels of corn.

"Zorro didn't chase crows," Tommy called. It pleased Duke to notice his dog tolerating Tommy for the first time. That told Duke there had been a change in the boy's demeanor. He snapped his fingers and Zorro bounded into the backseat. He specifically didn't tell the boys he'd see them the next day, and saw they both looked anxious. But he'd let their parents handle things.

He made a spur-of-the-moment decision to seek out Angie at her booth. As he entered the fairgrounds a volunteer handed him a map with locations and names of exhibitors. He was able to walk straight to where she was set up. Duke stopped a short distance away because to see her sent a flutter of pleasure through his chest and a sudden tightness to his groin. This morning she wore a blue shirt that matched her eyes, and her hair was clipped atop her head in some kind of fancy braid.

Her customer left, she glanced up, saw him and a smile lit her face. Luke, too, had spotted him and Zorro and came charging out of the booth. "Whatcha doin' here, Duke? T-Tommy called me this m-morning and 'pologized. Mom said that was the right thing to do. Do you think so, too?"

Duke noticed a slight slowing of Luke's normal run-on sentences today. "Tommy definitely owed you an apology. I came to see your mom for a minute, Luke. Do you want to read to Zorro? But we can't stay long."

Happy, Luke led the big dog to the back of the booth.

Angie came out, a frown creasing her brow. "Is the pony race still a go? I know Pam planned to see you this morning. I told her it was her call."

"That's what I came to say. We may have a solution. Pam and Gary are going to talk to Tommy then she'll call you. If all works out I'll conduct our final practice session tomorrow. If not, Luke will be terribly disappointed." His gaze cut to where his dog sat with his head across the boy's lap. "Those two have sure formed a bond." He laughed. "So much for Zorro being a one-man dog."

Angie smiled, because the term *bonding* had been bandied about a lot today. "It's good for Luke to read aloud and he does better with an audience. Dylan, I'm glad you dropped by. I couldn't get to sleep last night so I worked on the laptop. I love the website with the cartoon horse. I set it up, linked with a secure site where customers could pay, and this morning I already got two orders in."

"That's great," Duke said. "I can't tell you how glad I am to know you won't be working at the roadside stand anymore."

"You really are concerned about my welfare."

"I've been trying to get across how much I care for you, Angie."

"I'm really not ungrateful. It's just…I've had only me to count on in…well, too long. But, shame on me, I neglected to thank you for all the carrot and apple grating you did." She cleared her throat a few times as Duke continued to smile down at her. He caught her hands she waved around as she talked.

"I slept last night, and dreamed about you."

"Stop, you're embarrassing me."

"Where will you be at five? I can take my supper break about then," he said.

"I'll be at the shop. I have a high-school girl watching my booth the next two afternoons to give me more baking time. If you drop by I'll put you to work."

"It's a date," he said, slipping the word in so she'd get used to the idea of them dating. "I wanted to ask if it'd be okay to teach Luke how to do a flying pony mount." He quickly laid out the possibility he and the Marshalls had discussed about replacing Tommy.

Angie's eyes filled with concern.

Duke dusted his knuckles across her chin, tilted it up and brushed her lips with a soft kiss. "He'll be safe, I promise. And it will be a great confidence booster."

She agreed, maybe only because two men approached her booth.

Duke went to get Zorro. "Luke, we'll see you later today at the shop." It pleased him to see how excited that prospect made the boy.

Deciding to check out the other side of the fair on his way out, Duke spotted Colt's wife at a booth. He stopped to chat. "Is Colt due in tonight?"

"He is, and it feels like he's been gone a month. He loves handling the bucking horses for Thunder Ranch, but we hate the time apart."

"Doesn't absence make the heart grow fonder? I heard that someplace," Duke said, grinning. He picked up a silver cuff bracelet that caught his eye. It had a single blue stone in the center that was a dead ringer for the color of Angie's eyes.

Cheyenne Sundell, who'd finished helping another customer, came over. "That's a light lapis mined in

Montana. There isn't much of the vein in that color, which is why that cuff is so expensive. Customers all love it, but say it's overpriced."

Duke pulled out his wallet. "I'll take it." He still carried his portion in cash from the last purse he'd won.

Cheyenne wrapped the bracelet in tissue and tucked it in a bag. She took the hundred-dollar bill he gave her and handed him ten in change.

Leah studied him with surprise. "Am I missing someone in the family's birthday?"

"Nope." Duke thanked Cheyenne, took the bag, tipped his hat to the women and left, well aware he'd piqued Leah's curiosity. Probably he'd set himself up for Colt to cross-examine him this weekend at the rodeo. But if Angie came and sat with the family, maybe they'd spot the bracelet. *If she wears it. If she likes it.* Now he was antsy, wondering if giving Angie a gift of jewelry might be too intimate and presumptuous.

He'd worry about that later. If he began his workday early, he wouldn't feel guilty if he spent more time helping Angie later.

Dinah phoned him to say Pam Marshall had left him a message on their office answering machine to call her. "I hope all is okay with the boys being in the pony race. Another team in their age group scratched. Colby Martin fell off a hay wagon and broke his arm."

"If Pam solved things with Tommy, they're on board." Duke shared details on the kids' mix-up the night before. "By the way, I'm starting patrol early." He updated Dinah on the fact Angie had expanded her business, and mentioned he'd been helping.

"That's fantastic, Duke. I'm always delighted to see women-owned businesses do well. And Mom will be happy to see you two getting closer. Any news you care to report on that?"

Duke hesitated. "Actually, I am involved. And I hope she is, or can be. I could use some advice." He mentioned buying the bracelet from Cheyenne. "If I give Angie a gift for no reason, will I scare her off?"

"Are you kidding? Wow, Duke. I guess it's true what they say about still waters running deep."

"Now you're poking fun at me."

"No, no. It's a compliment. I'd feel special if anyone gave me one of Cheyenne's jewelry pieces."

"Ah, so can I put a bug in anyone's ear in particular?"

She sputtered enough to give Duke reason to wonder if Dinah did hanker after someone local.

His day started with a bang. He issued several speeding citations, mostly to cowboys anxious to reach Roundup fast to start partying. Duke knew that from now to the last event, his and Dinah's patrols would get busier even though it was great for the city's coffers.

Directly prior to his dinner hour, Duke ordered fried chicken to go from Sierra. She'd heard about him buying the bracelet and her teasing left him wanting to throttle Dinah or Leah or both. However, Sierra's ultimate approval removed his indecision about whether or not to give Angie the gift tonight. Jeez, gossip in this town spread faster than the first winter snowfall.

Angie had two massive bowls of horse treats mixed when Duke arrived at her store.

"I set the laptop on the counter so I can keep track of my cookies baking while you show me some ways to promote my website."

"I brought ready-made chicken dinners for all of us. But it's still light out. I left Zorro with Luke and gave him a Frisbee. I told him to stay between your shop and my pickup, if that's okay with you."

Angie appreciated that he was looking out for her son. "Luke gets so bored hanging out with me." She started dividing cookies into groups of six, preparing to bag them. "Pam called to say Tommy agreed to let Luke be the one to try and mount the running pony for their team."

"You don't sound okay about it."

"I worry how he'll feel if he fails. Add in my long-standing reservations about it being totally wrong to force animals to participate in rodeo events, and I'm not sure how I feel."

"Oh, hey, speaking of the rodeo events, I brought your tickets." He set them on the counter. "Aunt Sarah bought them, so don't think I'm forcing you to watch me ride," he said, laughing lightly.

"She did invite me to sit with her, Dylan," Angie said.

Duke loved that of all the people he knew only Angie called him by his given name. It sounded personal and affectionate falling from her kissable lips. He shifted his stance. He'd come to help her with business, not for monkey business. "I'll help bag the cool cookies while we talk about possible promo opportunities."

They worked well together, Angie noted.

"How much storage do you have for bags, mailing boxes, labels and such?" Duke asked.

"There's a big pantry. I need to keep the cookies as fresh as possible, so baking has to be done every day." She reached across Duke to replenish her stack of labels and for a moment her light perfume had him pausing to imagine burying his face against her neck where the scent seemed most concentrated.

"You finished your stacks," she said. "I'll be done with mine in a minute. Why don't you call Luke in to wash up, and I'll unload the next pans on the cooling racks. Afterward we can eat. I'm sure you want to eat before it's time to head back to work."

He did as she asked. By the time they sat at one of the tables in the outer room, Luke was full of stories about how Zorro retrieved the Frisbee.

They all laughed a lot. Angie and Duke chimed in with other funny stories. She found it was nice to have another adult—a male adult—sharing their meal. Luke reveled in the man's interest. And if she was honest, she'd admit Dylan Adams attracted her on many levels; more even than Carter Gray had. Yet, from the day he'd popped into her kitchen she'd tried to resist him. Tonight it was hard to name why.

"You'll need to arrange for a post-office box, Angie," Duke said, breaking into the place where her mind had drifted.

Angie shook herself mentally and got back to the conversation at hand. "First I want to put an ad in the paper for another cook. Or maybe I can hire you part-time," she teased, flashing Duke a grin. "Tonight we bagged enough cookies to get through two days at the fair."

"We could make it a family affair and I'd work free," he said, holding her with his eyes.

She flushed. "Ah, if I take some of this leftover chicken off the bones, can Luke feed Zorro?"

"Sure." He pulled out his pickup key. "Luke, his

water bowl is on the floor in the cab. Fill it for him, would you?"

"Okay." Luke grabbed the keys. "Mom, did you hear Duke say we could be a family?"

"Lucas…" Her tone held a warning. He screwed up his face, then dropped the subject and took off with the plate of bone-free chicken.

His departure left Angie rubbing at prickles that rose on her arms. "Dylan, Luke doesn't understand when you're teasing."

"I wasn't teasing, but I was testing the waters. Angie, surely you know I'm doing all I can to get close to you."

"I like you, Dylan. A lot. More than I expected to. And Luke's crazy about you. It's, well, you know my big issue. I won't ruin the enjoyment of tonight, repeating myself…but…"

Duke jumped in before she did just that. "All of that sounds positive to me, Angie. Before I take off, I've… uh… I have something for you." He dug in his pocket.

"Something other than the tickets?"

"This is something personal." He set the bag on the table and waited expectantly.

Her hand nervously bracketed her throat, but anticipation had her gazing at him with eyes wide.

"It's a little something I saw when I was leaving the fair this morning, and…well…the stone put me in mind of your eyes." He opened the bag and handed her the silver bracelet. "According to Cheyenne, the stone is light lapis, mined right here in Montana."

Angie's fingers shook and she almost dropped the bracelet even as her mouth fell open and she sounded similar to Luke as she stammered, "Dylan, th-thank you. It's—it's beautiful."

"I'm glad you think so," he said, his voice husky. She ran a finger over the blue stone, and Duke was moved to lean across the table to kiss her.

She brought her hands up to cup his face, and this time there was no question that she kissed him back. He rose from his chair, threaded his fingers under her hair and deepened the kiss.

They were fully involved when the door opened and Luke's shout broke them apart. "Duke, Zorro drank all of his water. Can he have more?"

Duke turned quickly, but not before satisfaction settled over him as he saw Angie a bit rumpled, but glowing from his kiss. "The chicken was probably saltier than his dog food, Luke. But he's probably had enough to drink. I need to go, so you can put the bowl back in my truck."

He lightly touched Angie's swollen pink mouth. "See you soon," he promised, then scooped up his hat and left.

Outside, Luke hooked a thumb in his front jeans pocket, and did his best to mimic Duke as he walked to the pickup.

Duke stopped and placed a hand on Luke's shoulder. "Tomorrow, I'm going to teach you how to make a running start and then leap on the pony's back."

"T-Tommy won't let Bobby or me do that."

"I think Tommy's changed his mind. He wants your team to have the best possible chance of winning."

"Really? C-cool. But what will my mom say?"

"She needs to talk to Mrs. Marshall, but I assured her I wouldn't let you do anything unsafe."

"Do you think I can get on the pony?"

"I do, Luke. I wouldn't propose it if I didn't think

you could. Tomorrow we'll see if Bobby and Tommy can slow the pony with the rope."

"Okay. If you say I can, I will." He flung his skinny arms around Duke's waist and hugged him hard.

Angie came outside intending to show Duke the bracelet she'd put on. As she stood in the doorway she saw her son's face tipped up as he eagerly gazed worshipfully at his taller companion. She felt such a kick in her chest she clutched a fist against her heart and suddenly had to blot tears from her eyes. The pair looked so much as if they belonged together it stole her breath. Unconsciously her finger stroked the blue stone Dylan said reminded him of her eyes. What woman could resist falling in love with a man that sensitive?

Unbidden, she imagined how such a man would be as a lover. Considerate. Attentive. Giving. Maybe riding bulls wasn't such a huge obstacle, she mused as Dylan left and her son raced back to the house yammering at the top of his lungs about getting to be the one to ride the pony in the upcoming pony race.

Chapter Eleven

The following week hurtled past at warp speed, it seemed to Duke. He fully meant to get back out to Angie's before Friday when the rodeo kicked off. Wednesday morning the three boys did so well in their new team configuration, for the first time he told them they could win their event if they didn't let the noise and the crowd spook them. Of course the kids swore they'd be cool.

Duke knew what effect a roaring crowd could have. He'd seen kids who froze and weren't able to move off the starting line and others who ran with the ponies, but forgot what the heck they were supposed to do. He waved them off to Pam's vehicle and returned to his deputy's job.

THE FAIR BROUGHT A LOT of visitors to town, but the rodeo broke all records. As well as cowboys converging from many states, area ranchers like the Harts figured prominently in many of the events. There were so many in the family who competed, and as often as not, won, so they tended to be rodeo favorites.

Friday morning, after stopping to talk to a few cowboys he knew from the circuit, Duke glimpsed his aunt

Sarah bustling about town. He excused himself from another bull rider and caught up to her as she left a bevy of old friends. "Aunt Sarah, you're looking pretty cheery today. Are things at the ranch improving?"

"I have to put on a good face, Duke. But the shadow cast by the loss of Midnight still looms over the weekend. I so hoped we'd have him back by now."

"I hear you. The heck of it is, little by little, stolen stuff is turning up. There's not been so much as a whiff of anyone putting out feelers to sell a horse. Dinah is beside herself to think the thieves are sharp enough to fly under our radar. If there is an upside to any of this it's that no new break-ins have happened since the fair opened, knock on wood," Duke added. "It could be because Dinah upped our patrol hours. Or they may be lying low until more ranchers come to town."

"I hope the weekend passes without incident, Duke. I do know at last week's ranch co-op meeting, we all discussed staggering our crews."

"I saw Colt and Dad bring in two stock carriers this morning. Do you know if Beau got home? Dinah signed him up to help with the Wild Pony Race this afternoon."

"Flynn spoke to him. Beau bought a new supply of leather in Great Falls. According to Flynn, Ace suggested Beau not leave the bundles at our ranch since so much of his lovely work was stolen. Flynn said he arranged to store the leather at Wright's Western Wear and Tack."

"Thanks. I'll hike down to Austin's shop and maybe catch Beau there. I wanted to let him know we can draw our first-round bulls this evening at six."

"If you miss him but I run into him, shall I tell him to call?"

"I would've thought he'd have done that already. He must have gotten sidetracked. You know he's been without a girlfriend for a while, but there are a lot of pretty women rolling into town for rodeo."

Sarah arched an eyebrow. "Speaking of pretty women, how are you getting on with Angie? I noticed Pam Marshall has been transporting the boys."

"Angie has a booth at the fair to sell her horse treats. She's selling a lot, and her online business is picking up. I helped her bag cookies the night I delivered the rodeo tickets you asked me to give her. I'm glad you invited her to sit with our family, Aunt Sarah."

"I can't help hoping she'll become part of our family," Sarah said, tilting her head saucily.

Duke bumped his hat down over his face, but mumbled, "Will it shock you to hear I'm on the same page?"

"That's wonderful. I'm happy for you, Duke. I'll stop at her booth, and we can arrange to meet and all go into the arena together."

"I'll see you later, then. Be sure you're on time for the Wild Pony Race. Luke's still afraid his mom will back out of going. I can't believe she'd miss supporting him."

"I know why she may want to skip watching him. I come from a long line of tough ranchers, but when my boys, Dinah, and you and Beau all entered junior rodeo I cringed. Many times I closed my eyes and John had to tell me if you'd all come out alive."

Duke laughed. "Here we thought you cheered us all the way. You were our rock whenever any of us got gored, stomped or ended up with broken bones."

"Yes, well, I learned to hide my queasiness. See that none of you get gored, stomped or break anything today."

"I'll do my best." He left, and it wasn't until an hour later that he tracked Beau down at the bull pens. The brothers did a quick male hug and slapped each other on the back.

"A nasty-looking group of bulls if ever I saw them," Beau reported. "Colt says a new contractor out of Miles City won the bid to provide bulls. They picked up some of Earl McKinley's stock, but some of these suckers came in from South America and have never performed before. I wish you'd told me. Now I don't have time to trace their lineage."

"I didn't know, Beau. Dinah and I have been working double shifts and trying to run down stolen property."

"Ace said there's no sign yet of Midnight."

"None, more's the pity."

"Austin said Dinah's losing weight over it." Beau took off his hat and raked a hand through his already messy hair. His hair was lighter brown than Duke's and had always been straighter. "Austin also said you've been wasting a lot of time chasing after Angie Barrington."

They both leaned casually on the fence, but Duke stiffened and straightened away sharply. "That's my business, Beau."

"Ouch. Touchy, touchy."

Duke yanked on his hat brim. "I hunted you up to remind you Dinah tapped us both to help with the Wild Pony Race at two. The three-to-six-year-olds are up first for the mutton bustin'. Colt and Austin are on board to help with that."

"What about Ace?"

"He's the official veterinarian on duty. If you hang out here for long you'll see him. He started early this morning certifying horses. He'll do steers for bulldog-ging and the bulls last. That's another thing, we draw our bulls at six at the announcer's cage."

"Gotcha! Where are you off to now? I'm meeting Shane Gillette at the Open Range for a rundown on what he's been doing down on the southern circuit. Care to join us?"

"Thanks, but I can't. I'm on the city's time clock all weekend. Sunday I'm doing my job and Dinah's because she's going to Billings for more workshops."

"I didn't see you registered for the Greeley rodeo, Duke. Did you forget that's where I'm headed next?"

"I skipped Greeley. I'll catch you in Casper, Wyo-ming."

"You're skipping a lot of events," Beau grumbled. "But I guess with your scores you can afford to pick and choose. Must be nice."

Duke slung a fake punch at Beau. "You're not doing so shabby. Well, *hasta luego*."

"Yeah, yeah. See you later."

Duke made an unscheduled run out around the pe-rimeter of town. He ambled down some ranch roads, to show a presence should anyone think about attempting break-ins. He parked next to Dinah's SUV at the arena about the time ticket holders for the afternoon events filed in to fill up the bleachers. Barkers hawked pea-nuts and cotton candy. The air smelled of fresh popcorn and spicy hot dogs.

"I scoured a few ranch roads," he told Dinah when he found her. "All looked quiet."

"Great. I wondered where you were. I walked in with Mom, Leah and the kids. Mom said she'd seen you earlier."

Duke craned his neck to see if Angie sat with the family. He didn't realize his stomach had balled up until he saw her and the knot unfurled. Then he couldn't hide his smile.

"What has you so happy?" Dinah asked.

He braced a boot on a fence and pointed to the arena where Colt, Austin and other cowboys plainly out of their element tried to get woolly sheep to cooperate. The littlest kids competing wore helmets. Each sheep and child had one handler assigned to help get the kid onto an animal's back and then sent the sheep toward the finish line. Many kids slid off. Some sheep refused to trot. The crowd roared with laughter, possibly because Colt's five-year-old stepdaughter, Jill, clung like a burr to her sheep. She passed a boy to win and Colt whooped, plainly proud of her.

"Everyone seems to be enjoying the Mutton Bustin' this year," Dinah said, chuckling.

"Yeah. Did you see Colt all puffed up?" Duke laughed, then added, "Looks like we're up next with the ponies."

Dinah rushed off to announce the names of contestants, and Duke vaulted the fence to meet his team.

"Calm down, guys," he said as he strapped on their helmets. "There's one group of younger kids before you. You are up against three teams in your age range."

"I know most of the kids," Tommy said, more nervous than usual.

The first teams started. Younger kids got the smallest ponies, but no child managed to get on. The crowd still laughed and clapped and the kids had a blast. All contestants got ribbons anyway.

"Okay, boys, block out the noise and concentrate

on staying with your pony." He traded high fives with each boy.

It was an odd thing, but as Sarah had said earlier, Duke was tempted to shut his eyes and not watch. He saw Angie had scooted to the edge of her seat.

At first the boys' pony got his head and Luke's short legs weren't gaining ground. Team four who had won the previous year began to act cocky. One of their rope-holders fell and lost his grip. Their runner dived for the pony but missed, so that team lost. Then, wonder of wonders, Tommy dug his boots into the mud, and so did Bobby, who actually sat down. It held their pony back long enough for Luke who, after two tries, scrambled on. Another boy on team two fell off the other side. Luke remained on longest, and so they won.

Duke delighted in watching Angie jump up and down. He pumped a fist in the air as the boys went to collect their trophies to a standing ovation.

To his profound surprise, while Bobby and Tommy raced straight to their parents to show off their trophies, Luke collected his and galloped up to Duke, throwing his muddy body into Duke's arms. Best of all, he didn't stutter a bit even in his full-blown excitement. Hugging Duke's neck, he said, "Thank you for my bestest day ever."

Duke carried Luke over to where Angie stood at the rail, her eyes aglow with pride. She kissed her son, then after Duke transferred Luke into her arms, she leaned over and gave Duke a big kiss, too. He was struck by the rightness of their little enclave. He felt like he supposed Colt did with his new family.

"Dylan, I wouldn't have believed those three boys

could win." She bounced on her toes, putting Duke in mind of Lucas.

He'd like to linger and vie for another kiss, but catcalls from Austin and Beau, who stood off to one side, had Duke feeling self-conscious. Anyway, Pam, Gary and their boys worked their way to where he stood with Angie, and they lavished praise on him, too. A bit embarrassed by the attention, he bowed out.

"I've gotta get going. Angie, you and Luke have tickets for tomorrow, too. Same seating. You'll have a closeup view of the opening parade and for all following events, including mine."

She hesitated, but Luke, still basking in his win, exclaimed, "I can't wait to come see all the real cowboys. You, too, huh, Mom?"

Though plainly Angie would opt out if she could, Sarah, Flynn and Leah arranged to meet her. The women made a big deal of the boys' win and Jill's accomplishment. And since they all included Angie in Saturday's plans, she finally said she'd be there.

Whistling happily, Duke sauntered off to find Dinah.

She left some friends, and added her kudos. "I have to admit, Duke, I thought you were wasting your time teaching that trio. We've probably never had a more crowd-pleasing kids' venue. The Mutton Bustin' was a hit. The rodeo committee asked me if the sheriff's office will sponsor it and the Wild Pony Races again next year. I should have asked you first, but I think a rodeo should offer something for a whole family, don't you?"

Duke thought about Angie's objections to the use of animals for rodeo entertainment, and he supposed the more animals they added the more she'd object. Unless he could convince her otherwise. "I'm sure the committee had to start early. If we accept, does it mean the rodeo committee will help you get reelected?"

Dina frowned. "I am so not looking forward to this campaign. I hate to think about all of the glad-handing that goes with running for reelection. I'd win automatically if we found those blasted thieves. Oh, by the way, I'm leaving before daylight Sunday. A guy in Bighorn thinks his wife bought him one of Beau's saddles on the black market. He's familiar with Beau's work. She bought the saddle from a friend of a friend, who picked it up cheap at a truck stop. If I can question the man who originally bought the saddle, I may finally get a description of a seller."

"Great. But we have enough family in town to watch for mischief makers. I don't expect our family to scatter until the rodeo closes."

"Beau told me he goes to Greeley next. He griped about you holding off until Casper. Is serving as my part-time deputy holding you back from what you'd rather be doing?"

"Absolutely not. I'm riding in all the events I need to make the finals. Beau's not as much of a homebody as I am."

"Your dad wants him to take over care of Thunder Ranch bulls. But Mom and Ace are debating giving up all cattle if Uncle Josh retires. Ace's practice has gotten busier and of course he has a baby due he hopes to spend more time with."

Duke knew part of the reason he hadn't signed up for Greeley was because he wanted to help Angie with her business. He'd never admit that to Dinah. "I can't imagine Dad lolling around doing nothing," he said instead.

"Well, he's getting older. So is Mom."

"A lot is changing with the family," Duke said, staring into the distance.

"Yeah. Thunder Ranch will soon be run by the next generation."

Dinah left Duke pondering that as she went off to see that rodeo goers left the parking lot in an orderly fashion.

At six Duke joined Beau and the other bull riders for the drawing of bulls. Beau's number came up first. He drew Nitroglycerin, one of the new bulls.

Duke picked next and got Tabasco.

"Man," Beau sympathized. "I don't envy you. Tabasco's a corker. Have you seen him buck?"

"Not that I recall," Duke said, listening to groans from other riders who weren't any happier with their draws.

"He's known for twisting one way then the other in quick succession, then kicking high with his hind legs to unseat his rider. I've seen him buck right out of the chute."

"Thanks for the warning. Shall we go have a look?"

Beau led the way to the pens. "This Nitro sucker is part Brahma." Beau's bull charged the fence, forcing the brothers to jump back.

"He's half-wild. Did you see his red eyes?" Duke said. The bull's coat was a creamy-tan. Duke's bull had a reddish coat fitting of his name. Tabasco bellowed and pawed the ground the minute they got near his pen.

"Let's go eat at the diner," Beau said. "Eat hearty, it could be our last supper. Those bulls look as if they could bring us both down."

"Pessimistic thought." Duke frowned. He wanted to

perform well—for the kids on his wild-pony team, he told himself. Really he hoped Angie would see he rode clean. But if Tabasco was a twister, handlers would badger him to strap on spurs for control.

It was a rare occurrence for the twins to get to eat a real meal together. Almost the minute they sat down, Beau zeroed in on Sierra Byrne and attempted to flirt with her. The diner owner, who often filled in as a waitress, didn't flirt back. Probably because the place was superbusy. Although, she appeared to not recognize them.

"What's with her?" Beau asked. "Is she trying to discourage cowboy trade?"

"She's probably run ragged. I imagine the diner's been swamped all day."

"Yeah." Beau sliced his chopped steak smothered in onions and approved with a happy sigh.

Duke noticed Beau tracked Sierra's movements as she delivered food to other tables. "She's not your usual type, Beau."

Beau jerked back to stare at his brother. "She has the most startling eyes is all. And what is my type?"

"Flashy. Sexy. Skinny." Duke cut his own steak and savored a bite.

"Huh. You have a skewed idea of what I like. Sierra is plenty curvy, though. Forget me and Sierra, that was quite a display you put on with Angie after the pony race. You'd better forget her, Duke. Haven't you heard guys on the circuit talk about her? She's a ballbuster, especially when it comes to rodeo jocks."

"I'm not a jock, and I don't want to hear disparaging comments about Angie. As a matter of fact, I need to get a to-go box and get back to work."

Standing, Duke peeled off bills for his half of the check and added another five in tip. He helped himself to a travel box that sat on the counter. "I've got the duty until midnight. Unless some huge mess comes up, I'll do my best to get to the arena to support Colt's and Austin's morning events."

"There's a party at the Open Range Saloon tonight starting at nine."

"It'll probably get pretty rowdy. Sure you want to go?"

"Not really. I told Dad I'd crash at the house tonight. He wants me to evaluate a bull he's thinking of selling. I should go straight to the ranch and skip the party."

Duke let his gaze roam the restaurant. "I'm surprised Pop's not here. Sierra told Dinah and me that he's been eating lunch or supper here almost every day."

"Our dad? Our nose-to-the-grindstone Pa?"

Duke gave a little snort. "That was my reaction. Pop and Sierra's aunt Jordan, who lives with her now, are old friends or something. I've seen them huddled together in a booth talking up a storm."

"Dad's got a girlfriend? Cool." Beau wiped his lips after downing the last of his cola, and added money to the stack Duke had left. The men put on their hats and moseyed to the door. Beau tipped his hat to Sierra as the two almost collided. She skidded to a stop and muttered an apology. He stepped out of her path, but not before he poured as much charm as possible into his smile.

"I don't know what to think of how Pop's carrying on, Beau," Duke said. "Miss Jordan is blind. Not that it's anything to hold against her, but instead of tying himself down, I think Pop should get out and have a good time. He's been tied to the ranch since Mom died."

"Do you think things are that serious between them? Maybe I'll get him to come here for breakfast tomorrow and see what I can find out." His eyes tracked Sierra as he ran into his brother's back.

"You should, Beau. Pop communicates better with you than with me."

Beau clamped a hand on Duke's shoulder. "As a kid, you spent so much time in a shell. Dad thought ignoring your speech problem was the way to help you get over it."

"Angie's son has the same problem I struggled with."

"Ah, that explains your involvement, then. Hey, my truck is back at the arena. I see you parked at your office. See you tomorrow." Beau loped off and Duke shot daggers at his back. Why didn't Beau get that he was interested in Angie Barrington as a woman?

Because he felt slightly miffed at his twin, Duke went into the office and phoned her. "Hi," he said, his irritation melting away the minute she spoke. "I'm on duty until midnight, but I wanted to call and see if Luke's come down from the clouds yet."

She laughed her tinkling-bell laugh that sent fingers of desire shooting through Duke's stomach. "He hasn't let go of that trophy even to eat," she said. "I hope it's made of sturdy material, because I'm pretty sure he plans to sleep with it."

"As all boys I know did with our initial junior-rodeo buckles. I slept with mine under my pillow until I won a second event, so I knew it wasn't a fluke."

"Now you must have a drawer full. Sarah spoke about how many events you guys have all won. But if you've won so many times, why keep competing?"

"You're forgetting the tidy sum that accompanies a win."

"I suppose. But I met plenty of cowboys who spent every dime they earned on entry fees and gas to get to the next rodeo. A shiftless life, if you ask me."

Her tone told Duke she hadn't softened toward his sport. "Listen, I need to run home and collect Zorro. I called to ask if I can buy you and Luke supper in town after the rodeo winds down tomorrow. The special at the diner is beef potpie."

"I don't know if we'll stick around that long, Dylan."

"I hope you will. Bull riding is the last event of the day."

"Oh. Then I suppose we can join you for supper."

Duke felt her tension rising, so he quickly said it was a date and hung up.

SATURDAY WAS THE MOST attended day at the rodeo. The stands filled up fast, and the arena hummed with activity as old friends met and picked their favorites to win.

Duke, like most cowboy contestants, pitched in to help with the various events. Sarah, Flynn and Leah, minus her kids today, had taken their seats. Duke kept watch for Angie and Luke's arrival.

He relaxed when he saw them wander in, clutching bags of popcorn and soft drinks.

Austin's bareback event was slated first thing after the parade led by the rodeo queen and her court. Luke's nose was level with the rail and he didn't move a muscle while trick riders and ropers performed in the parade. Duke thought Angie cracked her first smile at a spotted dog that rode in and did flips on the back of a Shetland pony.

Austin turned in a fair ride. It remained to be seen if his times held up and let him advance to where he could win money.

Ace and Beau stepped inside the arena and came to stand beside Duke during Colt's bronc-riding event.

Angie had scooted far back in her seat, causing Duke to chew the inside of his mouth. Colt never wore spurs, but some other bronc riders did. Duke sensed Angie's growing agitation, and then he remembered Luke's father was a champion in this field, which could account for her seeming displeasure.

Colt turned in an awesome ride. The family stood up and cheered. Luke bounced around, but Angie remained seated.

"Hey, Beau, I'm going out for a soda. Anyone want one?" Duke asked.

The others passed him cash and asked him to buy a six-pack of cola. Really he'd wanted a word with Angie. He went to visit her first.

Luke glanced up and spied Duke working his way toward them. "Duke, Duke, did Colt win? Will he get a trophy? When do we get to watch the bulls?"

Duke ruffled the boy's hair. "It sounds as if you're enjoying your first rodeo. What about your mom?" Duke asked, his eyes seeking Angie.

"Mom hates the guys who wear sharp things on their boots," Luke confided.

"Spurs. Yeah, well, fewer and fewer riders wear them," Duke told the boy.

"Too many still do," Angie shot back. "Why hasn't the practice been banned?"

Duke shrugged. He didn't know. "I'm off to the concession stand to buy sodas." He glanced at his watch.

"Bulldogging is next, then calf roping. There will be a break after that to let people visit the restroom and re-settle before handlers bring the bulls to the chutes." He pointed to chutes quite near where they sat. "Remember I said you two would get an up-close-and-personal view of my ride."

"What's your bull's name?" Luke asked.

"Tabasco. My brother's bull is Nitroglycerin. He rides before me."

"Those are funny names," Luke said, screwing up his face.

Angie frowned, so Duke beat a hasty retreat after accepting good wishes for him and Beau from all of the women except Angie.

He carried the cold drinks back into the arena. The men of Thunder Ranch huddled together watching other events and tabulating scores. Each had friends to root for.

Finally, after the break, the bulls were driven in. Duke rolled a second cold cola can over his forehead and winced because Tabasco gave his handlers a hard time. Beau nudged Duke and scowled. "Nitro is docile as Mary's little lamb. I don't want a rocking-chair ride, you know."

"Looks can be deceiving."

"The announcer reiterated that I ride fifth and you, seventh," Beau noted, turning back from watching the first bull up being shoved into his chute.

The rider, an out-of-towner, lasted less than two seconds on War Paint.

The next three didn't fare much better.

Beau's docile bull did not want to go into a chute. Handlers popped him on the backside, and Duke, Ace and Colt fanned their hats to herd him in even as Beau straddled the chute looking calm in the face of it all. He rode without a helmet or body vest in deference to the home crowd. Buckle bunnies lined up outside the fence giving him wolf whistles.

Beau gave a little bow and Duke rolled his eyes. He was continually amazed to think they shared a womb. Beau oozed charisma while Duke considered himself the no-nonsense sibling. Although, he'd observed a change in Beau this past year. He didn't party as much, he did more leatherwork and talked about something besides bull riding.

His bull turned out to be what was known in the business as a sleeper. Belatedly Nitroglycerin exploded out of the chute, went into the air and came down stiff-legged. He bucked in close to the fence forcing bystanders to leap back.

Duke heard Beau's leg slam into the wooden rails a split second before he lost his hold on the rope and was ejected into the air. Clowns moved in fast, but the bull managed to get his nose up under Beau's ribs and threw him a good ten feet back into the arena.

The men of Thunder Ranch dropped into the dusty arena and raced to help Beau escape even as handlers roped Nitroglycerin and manhandled him out the far gate.

Ace shoved his shoulder under Beau's good arm, literally half carrying him out. "What was my time?" Beau demanded through clenched teeth.

Duke, who'd seen Angie stand up, cover her mouth and then drop back into her seat, snapped at his brother. "Six-point-two seconds, but who gives a damn? Is your leg broke? Your shirt's ripped and your left arm is dripping blood all over from your 'rocking-chair ride.'"

They heard a howl go up from the stands and knew rider number six had taken a spill.

Ace tapped Duke's arm. "I'll get him to the first-aid station. You suit up. Wear padding and a face mask and helmet, for God's sake. Don't be a show-off idiot like your brother."

Beau made a rude gesture at Ace then tested his bad leg. "This paltry injury will get me gobs of sympathy, cousin."

Duke knew his brother tended to sound tough when he was in pain. He pretended to live on the edge. *On the edge of sanity,* Duke thought, tightening his chaps and donning all of the gear Ace recommended.

The first thing Tabasco did was try to crawl out over the top of the gate with both front legs. It was a good way for a bull to break a leg. Duke, who balanced gingerly atop the chute, spared a glance toward Angie. He thought she looked really sour. Luke, though, was a bundle of energy as he swung on the railing, taking in everything.

Handlers slapped Tabasco's nose until he dropped back into the chute. About the time Duke tried to settle on him, he bucked wildly. Handlers had to bring in two-by-fours to set across the top slats in order to force the angry bull down. Still, he banged around making it impossible for Duke to take his seat without smacking his legs on the chute sides before they even cleared the gate.

Suddenly as if tiring of the game, Tabasco quieted. He gave a little snort, tossed his head and closed his eyes as if he'd decided to take a nap. Indeed it seemed so to Duke, who wrapped his hand securely in the bull rope and gripped his knees against the bull's hot sides. He signaled and the gate swung open. Tabasco continued to stand like a statue. Handlers removed the two-by-fours and shouted at the bull and flapped their arms.

Duke heard the announcer remark that the bull was taking his sweet time coming out. He flashed another glance toward Angie and Luke, and saw her lean forward, bracing her elbows on her knees. Out of the corner of his eye he noticed a new handler arrive carrying a long, pointed stick. The kid suddenly and deliberately jabbed the stick in Tabasco's hindquarters. The bull bellowed and catapulted out of the chute.

Duke had time to see Angie jump up, grab Luke and begin dragging her son to the exit. Luke hung back, a deadweight on his mom's arm. But that was Duke's last glimpse. Then he had to focus all he could to hang on for the ride of his life.

True to Beau's warning, Tabasco twisted right, then left, then right, and each time he kicked high sending Duke sliding toward his neck and horns—that, while sawed off, could do major damage to a man's groin if a horn hooked him just right.

Duke felt his head snap backward and forward, and he thanked his lucky stars his face mask had a mouth guard or he probably would have cracked some teeth. Even though his heart sank when Angie marched out, his mind was in it to win it, and he kept his right arm circling high.

It was close, but he heard the buzzer an instant before he went flying over the bull's shaggy head. He felt the earth shake as Tabasco charged him. Duke's brain was rattled, and he wasn't sure which direction he needed to scramble to escape the snorting animal. Furious, the bull struck. Both of his front feet pinned Duke to the arena floor by the fringe of his chaps. Clowns and his friends moved in, waving their arms and shouting to distract the enraged bull. The slobbering animal pawed the ground long enough to allow Duke to crab walk out from under his big red belly that had already dislodged its clanging cowbell.

Colt and Austin reached down from the fence adjacent to the chute and hauled Duke unceremoniously up and out of harm's way.

His buddies all talked at once, shouting what a great ride he'd put in.

Ripping off his headgear and face mask, Duke stormed off to find the handler who still held the sharp stick. "That was totally uncalled for," Duke shouted, shoving the guy into the boards until Ace restrained him. "That bull's hindquarter is bleeding. He's so mad he could've killed me."

The stock contractor who owned Tabasco ran up. Duke stabbed a finger at the lamebrained handler. "I want him fired, or I'll report you all to the rodeo commissioner."

The contractor started to make excuses, but Ace, who stood between Duke and the stupid kid, held up a warning hand. "Raymond, no excuses! Your bull has a hole in his shank muscle. I'll give you some salve to use on it twice a day. But I'm taking him off the rodeo roster for at least two weeks. Your vet needs to certify he's fit to buck after that."

"Yes, sir," the contractor mumbled. Ace was well-known, well liked and spoke with authority when it came to the health of rodeo animals.

"Thanks, Ace." Duke calmed only marginally. "Uh,

Angie saw the incident where the bull got stuck, and she took off. I only caught a flash of her face. She's gonna be pissed. I need to see if I can catch her and explain that stuff never happens. I mean, it did happen, but it's once in a blue moon, and we…you dealt with the matter."

Ace eyed his cousin. "Go on. I'll listen for your stats while I grab a tube of salve for Raymond."

Chapter Twelve

Colt, Austin and a bandaged, limping Beau intercepted Duke as he charged toward the exit. "You stuck it out," Austin crowed. "I'm betting your time is a solid win. If you have a halfway decent ride tomorrow you'll be fully qualified for the finals."

Whooping, Colt tossed his hat in the air. Beau reached out to halt his twin. "You don't look as pleased as somebody in your boots ought to be about this news."

"You didn't see the handler who literally stabbed my bull and sent him into a frenzy?" Duke shook off Beau's hand. "Angie took off like she was on fire. She already has it in for our sport because she believes rodeo animals are abused. What that jerk did was prove her right. I'll see you later, I need to find her and tell her it was a fluke."

Looking irritated, Beau called after his retreating brother. "Forget her, Duke. She wants to believe the worst, so she will. You need to look over the field and pick a good bull for tomorrow. I recommend Bush-whacker." Beau's words flowed over Duke's back without checking his momentum.

Duke saw Dinah exit the arena. "Have you seen Angie?"

"I thought maybe her son had to go to the restroom at an inopportune time." As Duke started to jog away from her, she raised her voice. "I'm outta here for a week. Text me if anything comes up I need to know about."

Duke tossed a wave over his shoulder, but plowed on.

Sarah Hart bustled through the turnstile that led to the parking lot, as Duke was frantically eyeing the vehicles in hopes of spotting Angie. "Dinah, there you are," Sarah said. "I was afraid I had missed you. Will you run an eye over the grassy fields on either side of the highway between here and Billings? Midnight may be stashed right under our noses. What better spot to hide a horse than in a herd still feeding on summer grass?"

"I will, Mom. You take care, okay? Worry won't bring Midnight back."

Sarah nodded. "Duke, I didn't see you there. Fabulous ride. It's a crying shame Angie left early."

"Did she leave the arena?"

Sarah pointed to the parking area. "I saw her and Luke drive off when I went to look for Dinah. You seem anxious. Is everything okay with her and Luke?"

Duke unhooked his chaps on one side and dug out his cell phone. "Didn't you see that asinine handler jab my bull with a sharp stick?"

"The owner needs to reprimand him."

"He needs to be fired. Aunt Sarah, you know how Angie feels about mistreated rodeo stock. She was sitting near enough to see the blood running down the bull's leg. I'm afraid that's why she tore out acting mad." He had programmed her number into his cell and punched it now.

"Heavenly days, Duke, she wouldn't be mad at you.

You weren't to blame. Surely she understands you were on the receiving end of an angry bull."

Duke heard Angie's phone ring and ring. Suddenly it stopped. He guessed she'd seen his name on the caller ID and had shut the instrument off. *Damn!*

He rubbed at his neck which was already stiffening up from his hard plunge to earth.

"She'll come around," Sarah soothed. "You had a rough landing, Duke. Let Angie be for now. You go get a hot shower and a massage."

From the area Duke recently left, Beau whistled shrilly. He motioned to Duke with his uninjured arm. Austin signaled with both hands to indicate they needed Duke to come back into the arena. "I'd better go, Aunt Sarah. See you later."

He walked back to meet the others. "You, me and the Brazilian, Fernando Verdugas, turned in high scores," Beau said. "High enough to automatically qualify us to ride tomorrow. You get first pick of bulls, Duke. Let's go see what's available."

"Will you be able to ride tomorrow?" Duke studied his twin, who limped markedly.

Ace joined them. "You're lucky, Duke. Shoving that handler the way you did could have gotten you disqualified and/or fined. Flying off the handle is so unlike you. What gives?"

"He's acting crazy because Angie ran off in a huff," Austin supplied.

Beau made a face. "I can't believe, when you are so close to having the points to go to Vegas, you'd let a hysterical female jeopardize everything you've worked half your life to achieve. We're talking the bull-riding finals, man. The big daddy of championships!"

Duke thrust a stubborn jaw in his brother's face. "I swear you've shot off your mouth regarding Angie one too many times. I don't want to hear another word, okay?" He finished ripping off his chaps and tossed them over his shoulder. He stomped off leaving his brother, friend and cousin gaping after him.

Duke didn't want to pick a bull. To hell with riding the next day. He couldn't recall ever feeling so out of sorts. If love did this to a man, it sucked. *Whoa!*

Love? The word just popped into his head. What did a guy like him know about love? Duke only knew his heart hurt thinking Angie might close him out of her life forever over this incident.

He had to switch gears when a bunch of cowboys came by and congratulated him on his career-solidifying ride. It would have been the better if Angie had seen it that way; if she'd stayed to go celebrate with him at the Number 1 Diner as he'd asked her to. *Ah, hell!* He had to ride tomorrow. He owed his family—especially Ace, who'd helped out with the stock contractor today.

He reached the pens and accepted the stat sheet on the bulls that a rodeo manager gave him. Duke squeezed the bridge of his nose and counted to ten, then read the sheets. He studied the field and waffled between T-Bone and Mojo. Mojo was a black-and-white Criollo hybrid out of Chile. T-Bone was a brindle with an impressive lineage of bucking bulls in his background. Duke had ridden stock from both contractors before. Both were former bull riders.

Fernando Verdugas, who had chased Duke in the standings, also looked over the bulls. *"Amigo,"* he said, touching a finger to his hat brim. Duke acknowledged him back.

Hank Petre, the rodeo manager, addressed Duke. "You have enough points to take a bye on this ride if you want to. Probably your points from yesterday will hold to keep you in the money."

"Or not," Fernando ventured with a slow grin.

"This is the hometown crowd. Some come only to see guys ride who they grew up with. Put me down for T-Bone, Hank." Duke saw Beau and Austin making their way to the pens. He was still peeved at his brother, and needed to go cool off rather than have another showdown over Angie. "Good luck tomorrow," he told Fernando, and took off without knowing what bulls the Brazilian or Beau chose.

He left the rodeo grounds via another entrance and picked up Zorro before going to the office. He called Angie a half-dozen more times, and was surprised when she finally picked up.

"Angie, listen. Ace treated the bull. We asked to have the handler fired. I know you think stuff like that happens all the time. Really it doesn't."

"It happens often enough that I can't be serious about a man who plainly loves that world. This will hurt Luke, but please don't call or come by again until…unless you quit the rodeo. I'm sure that's unlikely, so this is goodbye, Dylan."

"No. Wait." But she was gone. He would've driven out to her ranch, except with Dinah away, all law-enforcement duties fell on him. And Saturday night of a rodeo and fair, that was when hard-drinking cowboys gathered at local saloons and let loose. As it happened, the first call from Ted, owner of the Open Range Saloon, came in as Duke debated going out to Angie's anyway.

The miscreants were two bulldoggers who'd won their afternoon event and then partied too heartily. Nobody on-site could say why they'd started an argument that turned into a brawl Ted had to break up.

"You knuckleheads," Duke admonished, cuffing them both before he led them, staggering, to his vehicle where he shoved them in the backseat. He put Zorro between them. The pair was so drunk they accused Duke of putting them in with a bear.

Back at the office he placed them in separate cells, then crossed the street to get them coffee from the diner. Returning, he wrote a report and made them shell out for damages.

Local bars were open until 2:00 a.m. The rowdiness continued. Duke knew there would be a lot of hungover cowboys at the arena Sunday.

He fed Zorro, and because he now had five cowboys overcrowding his cells, he ate a bag of stale peanuts and called that supper.

By midnight he resolved spending his night in his office chair. He thought about going home when the drunkest of the quintet started to howl at the brilliant August moon shining in their cell windows.

Finally, by morning, the cellmates were sober and a bit sheepish. Duke was tuckered out. Thank goodness this was the last day of the rodeo. He didn't think he could pull another all-night shift with no sleep.

Later at the arena he watched the stands fill. His aunt, Flynn and Leah filed in. Angie's and Luke's seats remained vacant. His heart felt like lead in his chest. He could still withdraw, but if he scratched now he'd forfeit money his aunt needed for the ranch. He was torn, but dang, he had to finish this event.

"I heard you had a full house at the jail last night." Beau sidled up to Duke.

"Yep." Duke knew the comment was Beau's way of patching up yesterday's discord. And he didn't have it in him to stay mad, especially when they were splitting up today and some of the family would hit the road. "How are your old bones today?" Duke asked. "I slept in the office chair all night, so if I turn in a passable ride it'll be pure luck."

"I'm hoping Sultan takes it easy on me. The doc put four stitches in my arm and bound up my leg after yesterday's fiasco. Guess I'll suit up in full-body armor today."

"Good luck here and in Greeley. I'm slated to help break down and haul off fair booths when this ends. I figure you'll head out right away?" Beau nodded and lightly punched Duke's arm. He knew their exchange was as close as either would come to an apology. It'd always been that way between them—a little touchy, but brothers all the same.

Passable rides were all either of them managed. Fernando won hands down, but Duke's high score from Saturday earned him the top purse. He accepted the money knowing he'd turn a good chunk over to his aunt.

Dinah phoned while he was in the middle of storing fair booths in a city warehouse. "It was Beau's saddle in Bighorn," she said without preamble. "The original purchaser said the man he bought the saddle from had it and three or four bridles at a truck stop. He didn't see a horse—or a vehicle. What struck him was that the young guy selling the saddle didn't look like a cowboy. He described him as a bit overweight. Blond hair, with a dark beard and mustache. It's not much, but the best we've got to date. Does that description ring any bells with you?"

"No, but I wish you had called earlier. Visiting cowboys are mostly gone. I'll post the description on our blog." He told Dinah about his night and said he planned to sleep eight hours straight.

She teased him about missing a Saturday night with Angie, and Duke admitted Angie had broken things off with him.

"Um, time to ask her out on another date. Or take her flowers. No woman can resist a man who brings her flowers."

He mulled that over and decided instead he'd try to enlist his aunt's help in putting in a good word for him next time she volunteered at the rescue ranch.

Surprisingly, when he saw his aunt a couple of days later, she said maybe he should let Angie alone awhile. "She took in two geldings rescued from the rodeo, Duke. Both had open sores from being whipped."

"How often does that happen, Aunt Sarah?"

"Never with us. I told Angie that, but she's not ready to listen."

"I guess I never paid attention to stock injuries before," he mused.

After he parted from his aunt he phoned Angie again. The minute she answered, he blurted quickly, "I'll give up bull riding. We're right together, Angie. I miss you so much it hurts. I want us to be a family, you, Luke and me."

The silence between them dragged until Duke's heart began to pound.

"Don't, Dylan. You know you can't quit when you're near as you are to competing in the finals."

Duke could hear her sniff back tears as she said, "I've heard that story about quitting before. Forgive me, but have you seen the newspaper? Photos of your ride made the front page. The whole town is counting on you to be Roundup's first national bull-riding champion. Please understand, the health of rodeo animals is serious business with me." She hung up abruptly, but something in her tone left Duke sensing she was as unhappy about ending their relationship as he was.

In the time it took him to drive home, feed Zorro and scramble eggs for supper, he was set in his mind what he had to do. He had ridden in his last rodeo.

He'd told Angie, but she didn't believe him.

He thought about people who'd feel he was letting them down. *Beau.* After rinsing his plate and sticking it in the dishwasher, he judged that Beau would have reached his destination for the night. Pacing the floor, he speed-dialed his brother.

"Hi," Beau said. "What's shaking? I made it as far as Buffalo. You caught me as I'm headed out for supper."

"I'm calling to tell you that as of tomorrow I'm canceling all future rides. I'm quitting rodeo, Beau. It's rodeo or Angie, and I choose her. I hope you can be happy for me."

"Happy? Are you nuts? I can't believe you'd let a woman lead you around by the nose, or that you'd blow off all the sacrifices I've made to get you within a few rides of winning a national championship."

"What are you talking about? What sacrifices have you made for me?" Duke demanded.

"Our whole lives I've done everything possible to build you up, to let you shine, because Dad ignored you so much. You asked why I let you win when we compete against each other. That's why…so you can be some-body important in your own right, instead of pretend-ing you're John effing Wayne."

"Hold it right there, Beau. When haven't I insisted you're the better rider? I'm a fan of John Wayne's mov-ies, yes, but I've never pretended to be a movie charac-ter. I don't live in a fantasy world, Beau. Furthermore, I didn't ask you or anyone to sacrifice one damned thing on my behalf. I'm sorry if you think I'm so pa-thetic." Duke shut off his phone, threw it on the table and stomped out to take Zorro for a run.

He was sure Beau would call again, and he was a long way from forgiving him.

An hour later he returned to his apartment, calmer, but sad, too, to see Beau hadn't called back to try and settle things between them. He hated knowing he'd caused a rift, but love for Angie gave him different priorities.

He rang Beau back, but his brother didn't pick up, so Duke attempted to explain. "Honestly, Beau, it never occurred to me the reason you didn't give your all when we rode in the same events was because you thought I needed you to lose to shore up my confidence. I wish I had known, because it'd probably be you going to Na-tional. You need to understand quitting is my decision alone. I don't want you blaming Angie."

THE NEXT MORNING HE CHECKED in at the office. No mes-sages came in and all in town appeared well. Getting back in his pickup, he drove to Thunder Ranch to see Ace.

"I'm leaving the rodeo," he told his cousin as they stood in Ace's clinic.

"Beau phoned. He said you think you're in love."

"I am in love. My aim, Ace, is to add to our family, not break it apart. I hope Beau will come to see that. If Angie will have me, I intend to marry her. I have an idea how to convince her. You've always been my sounding board, so I'd like to run it by you."

They talked until Ace's next appointment arrived. "I think what you propose is on the mark, Duke. If Angie can't see what a good man she's getting, she doesn't deserve you," was Ace's parting shot.

Next on Duke's list was canceling all of his scheduled bull rides. Once he did that, he swung past the newspaper office and arranged for his news to go in the paper's next edition. When all was said and done, he felt good and firm in his conviction that this was exactly the right move.

IN THE MORNING HE BOUGHT a paper, and was satisfied to see his news had again made the front page. Loading Zorro, he headed for Angie's to get down on bended knee. Unfortunately, on the way there he got a call from a neighbor down the road from her ranch.

"Sorry to bother you," Burt Mason said. "I know Dinah's gone. My barn was broken into and ransacked during the night. My wife got up before daylight to let the dog out. She doesn't see well without glasses and she'd left them on the bedside table. She tells me she heard a vehicle in our lane, but thought one of the rodeo visitors had missed the junction and had to turn around. I don't know why she didn't wake me then when she knows there have been break-ins. Honest folks don't think that way, I guess."

Duke sighed. He had no choice but to delay his mission. "I'm near your place, Burt. I'll stop and make out a report."

Mrs. Mason greeted Duke at the gate. "I feel foolish. Burt says I should have paid closer attention. I know the pickup wasn't new. It may have been black or blue or even dark maroon. The light and my eyesight were both poor."

"I understand. This is more information than Dinah or I have gotten to date. Every bit helps build a profile. What's missing? Tools and such?"

"Sacks of onions, potatoes, apples, and unopened wheat, oats and corn." Burt scratched his shaggy head. "Not stuff I've heard went missing from other ranches."

Duke's hand shook. Angie lived less than a mile away and these were the kinds of items she stored for her animals. Anxious to get to her place to make sure she hadn't been robbed, too, Duke thanked the couple and drove off. On the way, he phoned Dinah with the information. "Add these possible pickup colors to the description you got of the guy who sold one of Beau's saddles, and hopefully we're getting closer to finding these jerks. Do you think maybe they needed feed for Midnight?"

"Maybe. I'll be home tonight. Leave the report on my desk."

"Dinah, I'm headed to see Angie. I'll send this report to your iPhone. In about ten minutes I plan to do my level best to talk Angie into eloping with me today."

"You're kidding. I can't joke this early in the morning, Duke."

"I'm dead serious. I've quit rodeo, so you'd better get reelected so I can still be your deputy."

"Wow. Wow! All I can say is…congratulations."

"Thanks. You might say a prayer she'll say yes."

"What woman wouldn't count herself lucky to get a guy willing to change his life for her?"

Duke was more nervous after he hung up. Then he passed a field of wildflowers. Stopping, he picked a bunch of purple lupine and some dark red shooting stars. Before he could lose his nerve, he wrapped the flowers in the paper bearing his news and drove to Angie's ranch where thankfully all looked quiet.

He let Zorro out. The two of them approached her back door where he saw her in the kitchen through the screen. It reminded him of his first visit.

He knocked, but burst in before being invited. Also, as at his first visit, Angie stood behind her counter. This time she was making jam, not horse cookies.

"Dylan…I…uh… What are you doing here?" Her face was flushed, and Duke wasn't sure if it was from the hot jam or from his visit.

Luke hopped up from the kitchen table where he sat working on a puzzle. He raced over and threw his arms around Duke's legs. "Did you win at the rodeo and get a trophy like mine?" Luke asked, pointing to where his trophy prominently sat. "Mom said we wouldn't get ta see y-you a-again," he cried, falling into his old pattern of stuttering.

Duke squeezed Luke's shoulder. "I hope you get to see a lot of me." He had been rehearsing a speech from the time he left the Mason farm. Merely seeing Angie with her hair clipped up in a high ponytail, with color in her pretty cheeks, nearly buckled his knees. His fine speech flew right out the window. He said, instead, with raw emotion, "I'm counting on changing your mom's mind." Duke opened the morning paper and wildflowers rained on Angie's counter. "The flowers and news article are for you."

Her gaze left his face long enough to glance down. She clutched one of the shooting-star flowers and scanned the article, her eyes widened as she glanced up, still wary.

Empowered suddenly, Duke leaned over the counter and took her face between his hands. He kissed her and kept on kissing her until Luke smacked his leg and demanded to know what was going on.

Duke pulled back only far enough to stare lovingly into Angie's glazed eyes. "Well, Lucas, I hope your mother will allow me to help her finish up this batch of jam, and then she'll say yes to the four of us...her, you, me and Zorro...eloping."

Angie gasped.

Luke screwed up his face. "What's *'loping* m-m-mean?"

Duke started to answer, but Angie pressed the sweet-smelling flower over his lips. "Eloping means Dylan is asking me...uh, asking us to marry him."

"Hot diggity dog!" Luke fist pumped the air. "I told Bobby and T-Tommy that's what I prayed for at Sunday school. They said it'd never happen. Can I call them, Mom, can I?"

The adults smiled at his excited response.

Duke suggested he hold off a minute. He circled around the counter and took both of Angie's hands in one of his. "This is jumbled and I haven't properly said I love you, but I do. I want us to be a real family, Angie, but you have to want it, too. The last thing I'd ever do is guilt you into marrying me."

"We do w-wanna be a family," Luke yelled, tugging on both of them.

Angie turned shy. "I admit I fell hard for you, Dylan. Last night I hardly slept a wink for feeling awful about things I'd said to you on the phone. I planned to come see you today and apologize. I realized I care too much about you to be so selfish as to demand you give up bull riding, a sport you love, for me."

Duke kissed her again. Releasing her slowly, he said softly, "It's done and I'm happy with my decision. Very, very happy."

"So, can we 'lope r-right now?" Luke asked anxiously.

His mother murmured, "Is it even possible on such short notice? Oh, but we should marry in our church. And, Dylan, don't you want to wait and invite your family? There's your dad, your brother, Miss Sarah and oodles of cousins."

"Not if you're okay with it just being us. Some of them will be disappointed, but they'll get over it." At Angie's nod, he added, "I don't want to wait and plan something bigger. The kicker is, I can't leave town to take you on a honeymoon. There's been another robbery. They have to be solved. Since I'm not going to any more rodeos I'll have more time to spend trying to locate Midnight and return him to Thunder Ranch."

"We're okay with 'loping today, aren't we, Mom?" Luke insisted.

Angie nodded again, although she touched a hand to her hair and shed her apron almost dazedly. Gathering the flowers, she put them in an empty jam jar.

Duke dug out his cell phone. "May I have your phone book?"

She handed it over and he called the county courthouse to ask a few pertinent questions. Once he covered the mouthpiece. "At our ages, Angie, they'll waive the waiting period if you can prove you've had the measles vaccine."

"I have a certificate in my personal papers. But why only measles?"

Duke rubbed his jaw and tried to speak low enough to keep Luke from hearing. "The clerk said it's in case you get pregnant on our wedding night."

"Oh." Angie blushed and handed her cell phone to her son. "Luke, the Marshalls' number is programmed in. Go ahead…call your friends."

The next call Duke made was to the minister at their church who said he could accommodate them at two o'clock. That allowed time for Duke to buy the license, and change out of his uniform shirt into a new white one he had to buy along with new jeans to go with his Sunday boots.

Angie washed her hair. She found an almost forgotten blue dress in the back of her closet. "Does this look crappy with boots?" she asked when Duke returned.

"You'd look beautiful in feed sacks," he assured her even though Luke, who'd tried but couldn't tame his cowlick, made a wry face as he hustled the adults out to Duke's pickup.

ON THE DOT OF TWO, LUKE and Zorro witnessed Angie and Duke's vows, along with the minister's wife and daughter who were formal witnesses.

They didn't linger at the church once the service ended.

Driving back to Angie's ranch, she clutched their signed wedding license and her small bouquet of wildflowers, and smiled as she rubbed her thumb over a too-big, temporary ring Duke had put on her finger.

He noticed and was plainly perturbed at himself. "Angie, I'm sorry I didn't think of something as important as buying you rings. That high school class ring of mine is old and battered. I don't even remember how long ago I hooked it on with my pickup keys."

"I'm not sorry about one thing," she said, leaning her head on his shoulder. "I knew you were a man I could love when you brought me the laughing horse logo to help sell my horse cookies. I felt myself falling for you before, though, when we walked out to my horse pasture and you accepted Luke for himself.

Duke swung into a highway pull-out, set the brake and kissed his new wife thoroughly, lingering over the process to bunch his hands in her long, silky hair.

IN THE BACKSEAT, LUKE looped his arms around Zorro. With no sign of a stutter, he told the big dog solemnly, "I can't wait to start second grade, 'cause everybody at school will see I've got a mom and a dad. And a great dog," he added diplomatically.

* * * * *

The HARTS OF THE RODEO *miniseries continues next month with Shelley Galloway's book, AUSTIN: SECOND CHANCE COWBOY!*

ANGIE BARRINGTON'S HORSE TREATS

1 cup uncooked oats
1 cup flour
1 cup shredded carrots, or apples, or raisins, or
crushed peppermints for variety
1 teaspoon salt
1 teaspoon sugar
2 teaspoons vegetable oil
1/4 cup molasses

Mix all ingredients together. Form mixture into small balls and place on a greased cookie sheet.
Bake at 350° F for 15 minutes or until golden-brown.

REQUEST YOUR FREE BOOKS!

2 FREE NOVELS PLUS 2 *FREE GIFTS!*

Harlequin®

American ★ Romance®

LOVE, HOME & HAPPINESS

YES! Please send me 2 FREE Harlequin® American Romance® novels and my 2 FREE gifts (gifts are worth about $10). After receiving them, if I don't wish to receive any more books, I can return the shipping statement marked "cancel." If I don't cancel, I will receive 4 brand-new novels every month and be billed just $4.49 per book in the U.S. or $5.24 per book in Canada. That's a saving of at least 14% off the cover price! It's quite a bargain! Shipping and handling is just 50¢ per book in the U.S. and 75¢ per book in Canada.* I understand that accepting the 2 free books and gifts places me under no obligation to buy anything. I can always return a shipment and cancel at any time. Even if I never buy another book, the two free books and gifts are mine to keep forever.

154/354 HDN FEP2

Name   (PLEASE PRINT)

Address   Apt. #

City   State/Prov.   Zip/Postal Code

Signature (if under 18, a parent or guardian must sign)

Mail to the **Reader Service:**
IN U.S.A.: P.O. Box 1867, Buffalo, NY 14240-1867
IN CANADA: P.O. Box 609, Fort Erie, Ontario L2A 5X3

Not valid for current subscribers to Harlequin American Romance books.

Want to try two free books from another line?
Call 1-800-873-8635 or visit www.ReaderService.com.

* Terms and prices subject to change without notice. Prices do not include applicable taxes. Sales tax applicable in N.Y. Canadian residents will be charged applicable taxes. Offer not valid in Quebec. This offer is limited to one order per household. All orders subject to credit approval. Credit or debit balances in a customer's account(s) may be offset by any other outstanding balance owed by or to the customer. Please allow 4 to 6 weeks for delivery. Offer available while quantities last.

Your Privacy—The Reader Service is committed to protecting your privacy. Our Privacy Policy is available online at www.ReaderService.com or upon request from the Reader Service.

We make a portion of our mailing list available to reputable third parties that offer products we believe may interest you. If you prefer that we not exchange your name with third parties, or if you wish to clarify or modify your communication preferences, please visit us at www.ReaderService.com/consumerschoice or write to us at Reader Service Preference Service, P.O. Box 9062, Buffalo, NY 14269. Include your complete name and address.

*What happens when a Texas nanny learns she is
the biological daughter of a prince? Her rancher boss
steps in to help protect her from the paparazzi, but who
can protect her from her attraction to him?*

Read on for an excerpt of
A HOME FOR NOBODY'S PRINCESS
by USA TODAY bestselling author Leanne Banks.

Available October 2012

"This is out of control." Benjamin sighed. "Well, damn.
I guess I'm gonna have to be your fiancé."

Coco's jaw dropped. "What?"

"It won't be real," he said quickly, as much for himself
as for her. After the debacle of his relationship with Brooke,
the idea of an engagement nearly gave him hives. "It's just
for the sake of appearances until the insanity dies down.
This way it won't look like you're all alone and ready to have
someone take advantage of you. If someone approaches
you, then they'll have to deal with me, too."

She frowned. "I'm stronger than I seem," she said.

"I know you're strong. After what you went through for
your mom and helping Emma to settle down, I know you're
strong. But it's gotta be damn tiring to feel like you've
always got to be on guard."

Coco sighed and her shoulders slumped. "You're right
about that." She met his gaze with a wince. "Are you sure
you don't mind doing this?"

"It's just for a little while," he said. "You mentioned that
a fiancé would fix things a few minutes ago. I had to run it
through my brain. It seems like the right thing to do."

She gave a slow nod and bit her lip. "Hmm. But it would cut into your dating time."

Benjamin laughed. "That's not a big focus at the moment."

"It would be a huge relief for me," she admitted. "If you're sure you don't mind. And we'll break it off the second you feel inconvenienced."

"No problem," he said. "I'll spread the word. Should be all over the county by lunchtime. No one can know the truth. That's the only way this will work."

Coco took a deep breath and closed her eyes as if preparing to take a jump into deep water. "Okay" she said, and opened her eyes. "Let's do it."

Will Coco be able to carry out the charade?

Find out in Leanne Banks's new novel—
A HOME FOR NOBODY'S PRINCESS.

Available October 2012 from Harlequin® Special Edition®

Sometimes love strikes in the most unexpected circumstances...

Soon-to-be single mom Antonia Wright isn't looking
for romance, especially from a cowboy. But when
rancher and single father Clayton Traub rents a room
at Antonia's boardinghouse, Wright's Way, she isn't
prepared for the attraction that instantly sizzles between
them or the pain she sees in his big brown eyes.
Can Clay and Antonia trust their hearts and build the
family they've always dreamed of?

Don't miss

THE MAVERICK'S
READY-MADE FAMILY

by Brenda Harlen

Montana
★ **MAVERICKS**®
BACK IN THE SADDLE

Available this October from Harlequin® Special Edition®

www.Harlequin.com

HSE65697